Savage Night

I fear being a completely acceptable sheep in society.
-Marilyn Manson

Savage Night

Nicole Evans

Cover Illustrated by Kyrstin Sage McMaster

Library of Congress Control Number:		2010907507
ISBN:	Hardcover	978-1-4535-0903-6
	Softcover	978-1-4535-0902-9
	Ebook	978-1-4535-0904-3

To order additional copies of this book, contact:
Xlibris Corporation
1-888-795-4274
www.Xlibris.com
Orders@Xlibris.com
80315

Contents

Wear your past proudly; there isn't a reason to cover
who you are. Ignore the crowd that mocks you.
Be creative, be different, and don't conform to a
society that's destined to be like every other.

Thanks (insert your name here),
You've helped me with (something you've done for me),
I will never forget it unless I hit my head
really hard and it results in memory loss.

But really, thanks to everyone I love.
You know who you are.

*Special thanks to Kyrstin Sage McMaster
for the amazing artwork she did
to serve as the cover of the book,
as well as her many insightful suggestions.*

*And to the group, the first editors and
the people who've always had my back.*

Prologue

Fast-forward

"You won't hurt me," I whispered gently, too gently. Weakness seeped through my lips as I uttered those words, but I didn't care. Nothing could hurt me, I was with the only one I have ever loved, and ever could love. My blue eyes locked on his coal ones, I truly believed in my words. Why wouldn't I? He had given me no reason not to.

"Oh, but I will." And then he bit me. The fangs that had just been on top of my neck worked their way deeper into my thin flesh. The razor sharp edges pierced my skin like small knives, and then Chase began to drain me. Satisfying his thirst for blood, *my* blood, with no reservation. All I could do was stare past his brown hair in astonishment, while the life force that kept me alive was slowly being drained. It wasn't the first time having my blood taken, but normally all that happened was drinking, enough on its own. However this time along with blood being drawn from me, there was something being pushed back into my veins. Venom, probably; filling my body with it is the necessary action to make me a real blood bride.

"You will belong to me forever," he whispered in my ear. The venom's pain was nothing, hell, there was none. The bite? A mere prick, a sensual one at that, but those words set my heart ablaze with a fire that burned so hot it was a wonder I didn't die right there.

I slowly wrapped my arms around his shoulders, crying. It has been long, too long without this sense of relief, this sense of security. Never again would I have to worry about my place with him, Chase. My Chase. I'd never have to leave his side; we would live together and we would die together.

"I love you Chase, I always have, I always will." I pressed myself closer, if possible, to his warmth.

"Too bad I will never love you back." What? What did he just say? I blinked and loosened my grip on him. He couldn't have just said those words. No, it was impossible, he couldn't have, *wouldn't* have. Chase pulled me off of him, signaling that his craving had been resolved. He's holding my weak body up by the shoulders. Blood, which I had just sacrificed for him, dripped from his mouth, his fangs, and from the spot on my neck where he had bitten me.

"You will always belong to me, but I will never be yours, you will never have me. You won't even be given the pleasure of knowing you can ever be useful to me again stupid, filthy human. Did you really think that you were good enough to deserve the love of my kind?" He laughed, "You're an animal to our superiorority."

From his mouth that had once enveloped me tenderly now spewed vile words that hurt me with a pain I had never known to exist, then he let me drop. Nothing caught me; aside from the cold, hard concrete that he released me above.

"You see, Wynter, there are a few types of vampires," He went on, "As I hope you're catching on to by now. There is the normal type that eat, or rather drink, to survive, they rarely have human contacts. There are the kinds that want to help humans from evil vampires, like a certain friend of yours, and then there is my type of vampire. There aren't many of us left. We play this little game with humans, it's quite fun, really," His eyes were wide with excitement, "We spend an extended amount of time with one, such as yourself, and get them to fall completely and *madly* in love with us." He said this while placing an exaggerated hand over his heart, "As I've explained before, this would normally result in a blood bride bond where the two would live together like a married couple. However, the fun part of them game is turning said human into a blood bride, and then leaving them. *Forever.*"

My eyes widened, I had no clue what this was going to mean for me, for my life, what was life without Chase?

"You don't get it do you? Stupid, stupid human. You will live as long as a blood bride would with her mate, but that whole time *you will never be with me.*"

Then it clicked. Everything he had ever done all of the sudden fit together like a complex puzzle that created a picture you didn't expect. All these years I spent with him, everything he had done or said just brought us to this moment. I was, as he said, completely in love with him. The fun part for this sadistic bastard was telling me I was only a sport for him, while condemning me to live forever without the person I cared for most in this world. He gave me two hundred years of living, only to take himself away from me, my reason for living at all.

"Seeing you put it all together is fascinating to me. You're so young. I think this is the best job I've done so far. What's it feel like? Knowing that you have no choice but to live for so long, to watch everyone die around you, and not be able to turn to the one you love and know it was worth it? Everything I told you was a lie. All those years with me, just one giant lie."

He made everything nice and clear to me and I realized that I was mistaken before. The unbearably pleasurable heat that soared within me at first was now nothing. What I was feeling at this instant; well this was unadulterated pain. The earth shattered below me, above me, and all around me. I no longer felt any prick in my neck; I no longer felt anything at all, nothing, other than the pain of my heart.

"I never loved you." It was an aerial strike on my breathing; every lung movement came faster and shorter, making me dizzy. I was hyperventilating, screaming on the inside but not having enough air to make a sound on the outside. My face dropped and my heart was in my throat, beating faster, faster and faster still.

"N-never?" He leaned back on his feet letting out the biggest laugh at all, clutching his sides.

"You should see your face." And then he started backing up.

I know not of how long I lay there for, the only thing that I could see was Chase's smirk, the only thing I could hear was his further taunting about my destroyed future. Giving me one last look and a smile, he departed into the night, walking like he just conquered the world.

Nothing will ever be the same. He left. He left me! Just lying on the ground in the cold night. But I could not muster any anger. The pain in my heart and blood loss drowned out any other emotions that were sure to bubble up later.

Breaking, being torn apart by his steel fangs, anything would be better than this, why this? Everything was a lie; everything I had known was a lie. He had been my best friend, my constant, who could have seen it coming? What could I possible have done to deserve it?

Thinking that, though, I knew the answer: I loved him. I loved someone who seemed perfect to me, someone who meant the world, who I would give up anything and everyone for. Nothing good comes of that; the warnings are in all of the poems, all of the ballads. I chose to ignore them and this was my punishment.

Nobody will find me, I'll die here. I'll die here and I don't care. Humans were never meant to love vampires, we are of the day, and they are of the night. There's nothing left for me without him, Chase. No longer my Chase, but he never was mine to begin with, I suppose. He is his own, always was, and now I am his own as well.

~ ~ ~ ~ ~

I can't believe I fell for it, but I know that anyone else would have. I thought that I was different, that *he* was different. And as usual I found out the hard way that he's just like every other person I know. Only worse. He has all and every bit of me; I have no intention to take any of it back. Who else would I give it to? No one will have me now. Not that I'll trust another person, another *boy*, ever again.

Especially if he's a vampire.

1

What's To Come

And let me die before I wake,
For it was my soul, he did take,
And let me die here in my sleep,
Gave a monster, my soul to reap.
-Nicole Evans

I didn't wake up in a hospital. I woke up on the freezing ground, deserving nothing better. My head hurt . . . no, who was I kidding? Nothing hurt. I lifted myself off of the rough gravel of a park walkway, looking around. It must have been six in the morning, given the dew on the grass not too far from me and the sun's position in the sky. There was a dull throbbing in my neck; I reached up to feel it. There were two bumps, red I presumed, that were raised on my skin. Puncture wounds. Puncture wounds? Where did I-?

I stood up and the memories flooded back to me. Red blood, fangs, biting, something else, what was it? Why had Chase left me here? I agreed to this, I wanted it. To be his forever, his blood bride. His meal, his sustenance, and his lover. Then why did he leave me on the ground? I was forgetting something important, dark and foreboding thoughts lay just on the tip of my memory, what would have made him leave me?

"Too bad I will never love you back."

Oh God no, no, *no*! Everything came back to me now. The biting, the feeling of security, and then his words. Words that cut deeper than the sharpest knife, words that broke every bone in my body just for laughs. Everything, everything flooded back. Hot as molten lava, burning me up from the inside out until there couldn't be much left of this stupid being.

The swirls of memories brought on a dizziness that caused me to drop to the ground again. No one came to my aid because the only ones in the park at this time were the ones that lived here, having nowhere else to go. I must look like one of them, just another hung-over bum, lying on the street with nowhere to be.

I'm not! I wanted to scream. I wish I could. The burning pain in my lungs stopped me, my heart stopped me. I couldn't move anything; all I could do was lie on the ground and cry. Cry until I was completely dried up, then dry-heave until I broke down again.

A few joggers were passing around me by the time I snapped back to reality. Huffing and puffing, I could see their breath. Sniffling and looking up at well as I could, I looked around, I don't know how long I had been crying and staring off into space. But I was positive I looked high as a kite since the tears I cried would have turned my eyes red.

Groping around and feeling my head I considered that I needed medical attention. Chase drained me, and my emotions drained me.

I was dropped on the ground, and I had been sleeping in the snow since around nine, the time I went to meet Chase in the park the night before.

How do I not have hypothermia? How am I not dead on the outside? Must be because I dressed warm . . .

The few joggers that were out this early in the morning were giving me once over looks, and then averting their gaze before our eyes could meet, because if our eyes met then they would be obliged to help me.

I lifted my body enough to drag myself to a nearby bench and prop myself up against its leg. I saw the blood on the ground that had pooled around the wound on my neck and dripped down, then the smear where my hair had gotten into it and dragged it to where I was sitting now. Lucky for me my black hair wouldn't show the red in it; less scary for people to see.

I don't know how long it took but eventually a brown haired woman probably in her mid thirties got caught looking at me while I was looking at her, she sighed and slowed down, then bent over to assess my situation.

"Are you alright?" Was the clearly unworried question she asked. Her big and overpriced sunglasses reflected back at me, but I'm sure her eyes were uncaring as well. This was a hot spot for druggies to be, in the middle of the park on the most obscure path. I must just look like a prostitute that got banged up by her pimp. I saw myself in her sunglasses; I looked like I felt; a piece of shit.

Don't you see the blood? I tried to say, *the wound? I can't feel anything, but I've lost so much. No, I'm not all right, help me, he left me.* But all that came out was a sharp intake of breath, and more tears. The woman sighed again, I clearly was not the highlight of her morning thus far, I didn't care, everything was numb to me.

"Hold on," she said, "I'll call for some help, is that alright?" I managed a nod, or what she must have interpreted as one, for the next thing that the woman did was pull out her cell phone and dial 9-1-1.

"Hello? Yes hi, my name is Megan Parker; I'm calling from Nightingale Park" Megan, as I just learned her name was, turned around and whispered into her cell phone.

"Yes, I just walked upon a girl who was sitting on the ground leaning against a bench," A break for the response, "Yes, well I would say about sixteen," Megan turned back quickly to catch a glimpse of my face, trying to clarify my age, "That looks right, listen I'm where the people who do . . . bad things are." This woman wasn't going to be any help; she couldn't even say drugs, probably afraid the word would stain her pink jogging suit. *There are bigger problems going on here, do you know where Chase is? I've got to find him, tell him that I need him, where is he?* Nothing came out of my mouth, no words, no sounds, nothing.

"She looks alright, physically anyway. However there is a bit of blood on the ground, but I can't see where she's bleeding from . . . I think that she may have been roughed up by her dealer or something." Megan clearly didn't know that I could still hear her.

Help me, please! He went that way! I tried calling out again, still nothing.

"Yes, that would be wonderful; I'll stay with her until then, thank you. Bye now." Her cell snapped shut and the woman quickly turned to me.

"They're sending an ambulance, it will be here momentarily. You're lucky the hospital is right around the corner."

A hospital, that's where I need to be, right? No, that's wrong, what if Chase comes back for me? I need to find him! He wouldn't leave me here, never! He's on his way back! Oh they can't take me now! It has to have been a joke, a cruel, cruel joke! There was no game, but a test, perhaps! I've known him for so long, nobody does that to someone as close as we were, who could be that uncaring about someone's feelings?

And wait, aside from that, am I not a blood bride? What if they find out? They'll think I'm some sort of freak. *They could lock me away and Chase would never find me!*

"N-no." I managed to croak out.

"What?" Megan looked down at me again.

"No." I managed to get out, a little stronger.

"What do you mean 'no'?"

"Ch-ase. He-s coming back-k, for me, he lo-loves me, he promi-ised!" Sirens could be heard coming closer; I only had a little time to spare.

Standing up I regained my footing and wobbled away from where the woman was standing.

"Wait, stop! Where do you think you're going?" Megan called, catching up with me and grabbing me by the arm.

"Nobody's coming for you but the ambulance! There's no one that still cares for you at this point, I mean you were sleeping on the ground, humph!" Holding my arm, she watched me struggle to get away.

"Whoever left you here, left you here to *die.*"

The sentence was spat into my face, and again, I fell. I was reduced to curling into the fetal position, while I realized the truth in her cruel words.

"You will always belong to me, but I will never be yours, you will never have me. You won't even be given the pleasure of knowing you can ever be useful to me again, stupid, filthy human. Did you really think that you were good enough to deserve the love of a vampire?"

That was the first time I thought of death by my own hand.

"*No!!!*" An inhuman screech slashed its way through my lips as I clawed at my eyes with my nails.

"Stop it, stop it! What are you doing?" The woman tried to help me, then pulled back as I hit her off. By then the ambulance had arrived and one of the doctors had reached us. A man pulled her aside while another tried to calm me down.

"No!! He *left* me, I gave him *everything* and he's *gone*. Help me, I don't know anything, *help me*." I pulled at my blood soaked curls, dug my nails into my eyes, my face, and the arm of the man trying to help me. Any pain was better than the thought of him leaving me. I would tear my own flesh off, rather feel that then think of him.

"Miss, miss who hurt you? Stop doing this to yourself, miss!" Nothing he said stopped me and nothing he did could keep me from hurting myself in some way. The world was a blur, just swirls of color and his face right in the middle of it.

"George, George! Give her a muscle relaxant, hurry, before she claws her eyes out!" The man trying to hold me down shouted out to his partner. The partner ran to a medical box by the gurney and pulled something out of it. So many colors, my vision was unfocused.

"Are you sure we need to? Can't we just get her to the hospital and-"

"Give me the damn stuff, bloody need to, *yes* we need to!"

"*No! Don't give me that, I need to do this!*" The unearthly voice reaped out of me again.

"Just do it she must have OD'd on something, PCP by the looks of it, now give it here!" As the needle came closer and closer to me I fought harder and harder still. It took both men to restrain the wild beast that I had become and get the needle into my arm. Eventually, though, I felt a prick and the world seemed a whole lot calmer.

"She'll be fine, for now, let's load her into the bus and take her to the hospital." Were the fuzzy words that came out of one of the men's mouths. It was like being in a trance. Like staring off into space. You sort of knew what was going on, but not really. Not that it matters, because everything was dull. The pain, what had become of it?

"Stop it," I whispered, "I just want to see Chase, I miss him, I love him, I need him." But my words were lost to the haze that was blanketing my eyes, and soon the world around me was gone, vanished into a dark blanket that seemed to cover me. All I could think was incoherent thoughts, and all I could feel were the ever constantly falling snowflakes kissing my face.

2

Blind to You

I hope to God you'll be alright,
That you won't lose yourself to Night,
I hope to God you'll be okay,
And live to see the light of day.
-Nicole Evans

"Wyyynterrrr!" Someone jumped on my back, and whomever it was needed to get off *now*. "Wynter, Wynter, Wyyyntttterrrr!" I knew who it was.

"Shut up and *get off* Zelena!" I threw my best friend to the ground, tripped backwards, and fell onto her. Shit. Great, a few freshmen saw me trip, seniors weren't suppose to do that. I got up and coolly brushed myself off, sending them a glare, I was an upperclassman so I could do that. They ran off in a hurry, suckers.

"What's with the bad mood, *princess*? Pissed 'cause you can't see Chase until later?" Zelena tossed her dark brown waves over her shoulder and winked a chocolate eye at me.

"You know that's not the reason, you freak!" I said and helped her up. Pulling my curly hair she smiled up at me.

"Yes it is, and you're the freak for thinking that I don't know it!" So okay, that's all I think about, day in and day out, wanna rub it in? But despite my bad mood I had to smile. Zelena has this way about her that made you forget about being mad at all; it's a useful tactic when were dealing with adults, but just awful when it's being used against you.

"Just two hours left, then you can go home and see him. I still don't understand why he doesn't just transfer here anyway." Zelena continued.

"I don't either, I don't even really know anything about his school. Maybe it's advanced or something." I commented more to myself than to her, his school was one of the many mysteries about Chase. Being mysterious is one of his biggest traits, something that makes him both incredibly sexy, and incredibly annoying at the same time.

"So just ask him, you stalker!" Zelena raised her voice at me. I quickly clamped my hand over her mouth, looking around to see if anyone heard that, having a title of 'stalker' wouldn't be good.

"Zelena! God, I told you not to call me that! And I don't stalk him!" I snapped at her, my anger management control was wavering. I loved her, but boy, she was infuriating. "I've only tried to follow him home once, and that's because I wanna see where he lives!" Oh damn, isn't that the definition of stalking?

"For the record, there's nothing closer to stalking than that," Zelena confirmed.

I whined, "Well it's just like, he knows where I live, where I go to school, my favorite foods, colors, hobbies, he knows *everything* about me, but I know nothing about him. For God's sake I don't even know where the guy lives! So it's not stalking. Can we please just call it data collecting or something?"

We continued our banter on whether I was a stalker or not, but Zelena could probably tell that I wasn't into it, 'cause she went to class and said we could talk later, knowing I wouldn't be in school much longer.

The weather was perfect, no sun and overcast. It had just rained a little before and it was still drizzling now, the air was cool. On days like this, Chase's and my favorite kind of day, I normally get more restless than usual, and end up skipping the second half of the day. Zelena used to try to make me stay, but soon realized that if I wanted out, I was gone.

It wasn't so much that I was skipping that she had a problem with, as much as she didn't like Chase. He didn't show up when she was there, and left if she was coming, always missing her. His excuse was that he didn't want people to know him, he was shy, or that he was busy. I knew that was a lie, and he knew I knew that. But I never bothered correcting him or asking for the real reason, knowing well that he wouldn't give it.

Minutes after parting ways with Zelena I grabbed my coat from my locker and ran out the door. Someone was calling, but I chose to ignore it, they won't remember. If they did, who cares, what are they going to do, call my home?

Breathing in the wet air I dashed to the woods by my house, which would be empty, like always. Half the reason I could do things like this, skipping so often, is because I'm aware that the house will always be desolate.

My parents sort of got up and left when I was thirteen. My aunt tells me that they were never bound for a settled life, and I don't blame them. I raised myself, or my aunt helped once in a while. She took over as my guardian but only gets involved when adults come looking for her. I like to be on my own with the exception of Zelena, and of course Chase.

I couldn't wait to see him; he'd be where we meet up around when I would be. It's an unspoken rule that we both ditched when the weather was like this, if we could, and I don't remember a time we haven't been able to.

Our meeting spot was only a few miles away from the school, not a far walk really. I would just start walking home then turn off the road into the woods at some point. I live in a small town so no cars go by.

The trees above me kept dropping the rain that collected on its leaves, leaving me in a great mood, and soon to be better. Chase had to be there first, he normally was, even if I took a car he'd still be there first. It was yet another mystery as to how he did it, but I didn't care. As long as he gets there, that's all that matters.

The first day we met was perfect like this one. I was taking a walk on the street near my house and went off into the woods, after school of course. I was a good kid back then, never missed a day of class, so my adventures were always in the afternoon. When I came across a pond pretty deep into the woods, I thought that it was a fairytale set up just for me. A place I could sit and think, do homework perhaps. There was this amazing climbing tree right next to it and the pond was surrounded by other trees right along its banks. No clearing, which was amazing, I don't like big open spaces. I thought it could be my own, but I was wrong.

I fell asleep under the climbing tree in the drizzly rain and when I woke up there was a beautiful boy lying not too far from me. Long story short, it was Chase. Apparently I had stepped into his favorite place, but since then we've shared it.

Exiting the memories in my head I tried to climb the wet tree too fast, but I was all giddy from thinking about Chase I missed a limb and fell on my butt.

"It's a good thing Chase didn't see that," I commented to myself. I got up and brushed wet dirt off of myself, an impossible think to do.

I have a habit of talking to myself. Most people find that weird, but I think it's useful. After I put my jacket on the ground I then set to the task of trying to get a now set in mud stain out of the front of my skirt. That's when Chase dropped down gracefully from the tree in front of me. His lean six-foot frame blocked my view of the pond.

"I thought I'd give you time to, um, clean up." Came his gravely voice, "But it looks like you've got another stain, again. Really Wynter what have I said about running up a tree?" He joked in a playful way.

"Well I just love this weather so much I guess I'm going too fast to get to where I can enjoy it." I replied, knowing what he would ask next.

He smirked, "And the other reason?"

I bit down a blush, not wanting him to see me like that, "And 'cause I wanted to see you too, Chase, you know that, no need to ask." His smirk grew.

"Yeah I know, but I like hearing it anyway." I melted into the ground, like I do every time he talks.

"Well, c'mon over here Wynter!"

Looking at him then back at my wet and dirty clothes I shrugged, "I'm all dirty, I don't want to get you muddy too."

In two of his long strides Chase came to where I was standing and wrapped me in a hug, "Stupid, I don't care about getting dirty, I haven't seen you since yesterday, I missed you." Hard not to fall in love with that, am I right? Stepping back I looked at his face, to refresh the image. His hard coal eyes looked back at me. They're foreboding to some I imagine, but to me they were as perfect as his lips, his arms, his chest, and mostly, his smile.

His smile was the most brilliant thing I've ever seen, though he never did it enough, not enough for me at least. Whenever he's happy enough to smile I notice that he always has to turn and face the other way, or distracts me in some way. Him smiling is my favorite thing ever, and even if I don't see him do it, I want to make sure that it's always there.

"I missed you too, Chase," I replied, pulling him into another hug, "Have you been waiting here long?" He pulled me onto the grass before answering, knowing by now that I didn't care about dirty clothes as long as the day was like this and we were together.

"Not too long, I knew you were coming." Came his nonchalant answer.

"How?" I sat facing him, hoping that he would answer this one question for me.

He rolled his eyes, "You're pretty predictable, Wynter." He talked as if it were the most obvious thing in the world

"Hey," I said, poking him in the chest, "I want to inform you that I am in no way predictable! And you're not suppose to say that to someone like me anyway!" Chase lay down on his back, arms behind his head, seeming perfectly content.

"You are, in fact, very predictable." Retorted the boy laying near me.

"Hah! Bullshit. Try something, anything, I bet you won't be able to guess what I'll do." I normally won in challenges like this against other people; I was pretty out there both in actions and thoughts.

"Okay then," He said, turning to me, "Close your eyes and picture this." I did as he told me to, preparing my mind to have the complete opposite reaction that a normal person would expect.

"Just think of me . . . naked." My face heated up about a thousand degrees over what it was supposed to be and my eyes popped open.

"You dick!!" I hit his chest, "Man that *so* doesn't count and you know it!" I hit him again before turning the other way, trying to turn back to my normal pale color. Red showed up very easily on me.

"Don't hide that face, it's okay to blush. I know I would too if I imagined something as attractive as that." He grinned a closed mouth evil grin and mimicked me.

"I did not. I was just embarrassed by the fact that you wanted me to think of that." Even though I did think of . . . *that*. Just for a second. Really, I would have thought of it all day.

"Whatever you say, Wynter, whatever you say." I mumbled but there wasn't much use denying it. You can't help but picture something that someone tells you to. (A dog in a tutu. See? Did you not just imagine that?)

I huffed and lay down next to him. I stared at the sky and every so often a drop of rain would kiss my face. Words never really needed to be passed between us, it was an easy friendship, it came naturally. That was one of the reasons I couldn't tell him how I felt unless I was positive he felt the same way. What we had was too much to ruin over petty feelings.

I felt him pull my long hair, playing with one of my natural banana curls, and I moved a little closer to allow him to do so. Chase was never demanding. Some friendships like this the guy expects to do stuff with the girl because, well I don't know why, because it would be convenient I suppose. But simply playing with a strand of hair seemed enough for him, even though we both know that I would do anything he told me to. Chase was a gentleman.

Thus far it was a normal day for the two of us, just sitting or lying down, talking or not. Just hanging out was fun enough and the time flew.

But no matter what we were doing, his action always ended up with my neck. At some point when we hang out he always brings some sort of attention to it. When we first met he surprised me by staring at my neck, in lieu of my boobs. By the time I considered him to be my best friend, he had moved on to a touch which could be perceived as accidental, but wasn't. Some days he gently brushed the skin, moving my hair; and other days he would go as far as to breathe on it. Almost a kiss, but not quite.

Chase sat up and leaned against the tree, pulling me halfway onto his lap as he did so. We're friends, friends do this sort of stuff, am I wrong? I know no different, seeing as though he's my only guy friend. I used to have more, but there was too much pressure to be a 'normal' girl, who giggles and flirts with everyone until I was tied down.

I closed my eyes and Chase continued to pull at my hair and tuck it behind my ears, his fingertips lightly caressed my neck. It always sent shivers up and down my spine when he did that.

Every so often there was a little more touching. He pushed me a little further until I wasn't sure I could take it without jumping the guy; which I had thought of doing on more than one occasion. Nothing that was overly inappropriate, but I mean if I could just secure a kiss with him, that would make it better. I'm not sure if this is his subtle way of telling me he may like me back, but it still wasn't worth the chance.

My eyes were still closed as he took my head in between his two hands and tilted it to the right. I felt him breathing on the inside of my ear, sending such chills up my spine that I had to hold onto his shirt to keep myself from squirming. I opened my eyes, feeling him stop moving, to see him staring directly into mine. Coal met blue and I fell into a vortex that I wouldn't want to come out of if my life depended on it. Then he averted his gaze and pressed his lips right where my cheekbone met the top of my neck.

It was the first time his lips had touched any part of me, and I didn't even care that it wasn't my own lips; this was thrilling by itself. It happened so fast, it wasn't anything like I imagined it to be. I thought it would be different in some way, but this was better than anything I could have dreamed.

I closed my eyes and concentrated on keeping this feeling as long as I could. The sexiest most beautiful and caring being ever to walk on this earth was kissing my neck. The way he did it was like he was looking right into my soul but through my skin. I didn't care about anything else going on in the world, only that Chase was kissing some part of me. He could have been the most evil person in the world, and I wouldn't care. I was blinded by love, nothing mattered to me accept him.

But I knew that he was nothing but the best, the most wonderfully sweet, person ever to live. He had to be, he was my Chase.

3

Watching and Waiting

A dead rose holds no meaning,
Folded over a thousand prayers.
Wilted, dying, un-savable,
The color has faded to black.
-Nicole Evans

The next day there was a scrape on my neck. Looking into the mirror on the bathroom wall I noticed it. It wasn't a hickey or a bite mark or anything, it looked like a weird paper cut. Not from Chase, his lips sure as hell couldn't do that. And teeth aren't that sharp.

How am I going to explain this to Zelena? She has like super eyesight or something; she'll see it for sure. I thought to myself. No matter, I could just wear a choker necklace to cover it up. Pulling the black silk around my neck I realized that it didn't cover the small cut, not even just a little. *Dammit, Zelena isn't going to believe it's a cut. It couldn't be from Chase but she won't buy that. How did I cut myself anyway? I probably got it when I fell, maybe that's why Chase kissed it. Yeah, he doesn't like me; it's 'cause of this cut . . .*

As I was coming out of the bathroom I got the feeling that I was being watched. Out of the corner of my eye there was a black figure standing on the tree outside my window, making a soft tapping to be let it.

"Oh, kitten! Did I leave you in the rain?" It was my little Russian Blue, pawing at the window, "Oh I'm sorry little one, here, I'll let you in!" After opening the window, a hand grabbed Nightmare, which was her name, and swung into my room with her in tow. Trying to make room for whoever it was coming in I backed up and tripped over a pile of clothes I left in the middle of my room, like always, and landed on my butt, something I did a lot.

"Jeez Chase why can't you use the door like normal people do?" I screeched, "You scared me half to death!"

Completely ignoring my question, "How's Nightmare doing?" He asked, scratching her head, earning a content noise rolling off of her.

I stood up, finding no use in sitting on the ground, then tried to clean my room best I could. So really just pushing clothes out of the way.

"She's doing good, bigger since you last saw her, right?"

"Considering that I see her close to every night, no, not by much." Chase let her drop down and sat on my unmade bed.

"Very funny, but the last time you were over here was a week ago." I said, still attempting to clean my room.

"That you know of, maybe I sit in that tree and watch you all night." Chase said in an I'm-a-creepy-stalker voice.

"Harde har har. It would take a seriously weird person to watch a girl sleep all night. Zelena's friend Ed did that when his girlfriend Bell slept. That relationship ended up sort of weird." I trailed off, sending a black book flying in the back of my room. I would have to go back and get it later. Some things just aren't meant to stay in the closet, where it landed.

"Maybe I should call the police though, to investigate that, just incase." I teased. His face started to form a grin, which he promptly covered up, naturally.

"Oh, I know you wouldn't." He said, lowering his hand now that he had contained himself.

"Wouldn't what? Call the police? And how do you know that?"

"You'd never do anything that I don't want you to!" He was smiling, but his eyes looked serious, demanding almost. I inwardly gasped, stepping back a little. Sure we both knew that little piece of information was a fact, but it was one of those things that we silently agreed not to bring up. For the sake that I would be immensely embarrassed and he would feel, well actually it may have just been for my sake.

"N-no, I do whatever I want! You have no power over me!" I retorted back at him. Standing my ground. There was no way I was going to openly admit that to him, it was far to embarrassing.

"I didn't see you trying to stop me yesterday." That caught me off guard, that and the gleam in his eyes, telling me that I shouldn't respond. That gleam told me that it was a trap, but I ignored it, thinking that it was my imagination.

"Well you still have no power over me I could have made you stop if I wanted to!" I belted out without thinking. Then I thought. *Oops*.

"If you wanted to, eh?" Came the reply. So that gleam did mean something. Egotistic bastard.

"Wel-l I was-uh-just um, what I mea-nt to s-say was tha-t," I trailed off, feeling the heat rising up my neck; and then he was standing up, walking toward me. I backed up until I felt the poster-covered wall of my room stop me. Chase's hands were immediately on either side of my head, effectively trapping me where I was.

"What did you mean to say then, Wynter?"

I had no response to that, feeling that I had dug my grave, and probably shouldn't make it any deeper; I kept my mouth closed.

Slowly, his head started descending to my level, his eyes on my lips.

Kiss me. Kiss me. Kiss me! I couldn't help but shout in my head. He had me expecting it, coming this close after what happened yesterday.

I wished as hard as I could, hoping that my mind could make him obey. Then, as if listening in on my thoughts, his face was right in front of mine. I closed my eyes and lifted my face up at a better angle.

Right when I should have felt his lips on mine, I heard his breathing in my ear.

"You know, you're going to be late for school at this rate." Blue eyes popped open to see black ones retreating.

"I, but you, argh, *Chase*!" Fuming didn't even begin to describe what I was feeling right now, he didn't kiss me today, he made fun me, though that was normal, and now I was going to be late for school!

"We'll talk about this later!" I screamed, getting the rest of my stuff together and running out the bedroom door. As soon as I locked my house door I yelled up to where my room was.

"And get outta my house, go to school for once!"

"You should be talking Wynter!" Came the faint reply out of my window.

Bolting to school, I had missed the bus by then, I knew that I was going to be late, again, but it didn't matter to me all that much.

Stupid Chase, teasing me like that. I really wanted him to kiss me . . . oh well, whatever it'll happen someday.

I hope.

~ ~ ~ ~ ~

When I got to school I was surprised to find that I was only a little late, for me, and it was only gym. In the locker room I threw the uniform on and snuck into class, joining my running classmates. Lucky for me, Zelena was among those people in my class. I ran up to her, wanting to catch up on what I had missed in US history, one of the classes I had skipped yesterday.

"Hey, hey, hey Lena!"

"Wynter? Hi!" After the initial shock of seeing me a quizzical look crossed her face, "I thought you were gonna end up ditching today too, the weathers great, well, according to you anyway."

"Yeah, I'll probably head out early, I have study last today, but I don't wanna get in too much trouble." I explained in between breaths. Zelena just gave me one of her looks.

"Okay, okay yeah you're right I don't care but still, I just kinda don't wanna see Chase right now."

As soon as the words were out of my mouth Zelena stopped running and grabbed each of my shoulders.

"What did he do?" Was the demanding question. A hard look had crossed her face, she was pretty pissed off, but not at me, I could see the concern there too, but boy if Chase were here right now, he'd be dead.

"Nothing, nothing, he didn't do anything bad! Promise!" Zelena narrowed her eyes and did a once over of the skin she could see, making sure I didn't have any bruises that could have been caused by him. Everything seemed to check out by her, so I let out a sigh, until I saw her eyes land on my neck, and widen to the size of, well, big eyes.

"No, no it's not like that, I fell outta a tree! Seriously, I did." I ran backwards trying to explain so that she would believe me. It was the truth, after all.

"Is that a hickey? No, it's not. What is that thing?" She saw herself that it wasn't a hickey, but it was still a cut, no matter how small. That wasn't going to make her like Chase at all. Even if it wasn't his fault.

"I went to where we meet and tried to climb a tree too fast, slipped, and I guess that's how I got this." I explained further. She rolled her eyes because my story was oh-so-believable.

"Look, Wyn," She sighed, "I'm just worried for you. I don't know him and you don't know him as well as you think you do." I opened my mouth to respond, to tell her that I did in fact know him, only to close it, realizing that I really didn't.

"The only way I'm going to stop terrorizing you about him is if he agrees to meet me. How long has it been? Like four years or something?" I guess she was putting her foot down on this one. The look on her face was pure absolution.

I let out a sigh, Chase wasn't gonna like this one.

"Look it's just a little cut for God's sake." Her insisting was irking me.

"It's not that, you're my best friend and I'm yours. If you have someone like that in your life, why can't I meet him?"

I sighed and gave up, "Fine, come with me to my house from study, can you skip last period?" Zelena bit her lip, a sign that she was thinking, probably trying to figure out what she had last. She wasn't big on skipping class.

"Oh, yeah, I have cooking, nothing drastically important."

"I suppose I'll just meet you outside then, say you have study too, they'll let us go, right?"

"Yeah, since we're seniors. Not that it matters to you."

"True."

Chase was *not* going to like this.

~~~~~

The rain had not yet begun when Zelena and I walked out the school gates, but it was coming, and it felt like a storm. The weather report for this week was drizzly with the possibility of a thundershower. A nice change, it was sunny here too often. I hate the sun, I burn quite easily.

"So where are we going?"

"Well I don't wanna take you to where we normally meet up, it's kind of a secret place for us," I trailed off. There was no way I would take her there, it was much too personal, too private, for another person. It would just shatter it in my mind.

"That's okay, just where though?"

"He always kind of knows where I am, I'm not sure why," At this comment Zelena raised an eyebrow but refrained from asking anything, "Anyways," I continued, "I'm sure he'll find us, if we don't find him first. Lets go to my house before anything though, okay?"

"Fine by me, it's your plan." A simple reply to what I had tried to explain to her.

It took longer than normal to get home, Zelena was lazy and a slow walker, it started to rain, but we continued to take our time. The light blue house I lived in was in view when it started to really come down, like I thought it would. *My flowers are going to drown,* I thought.

Ignoring my poor plants, "Sometimes we meet in my room when it's just too rainy to go outside, maybe he'll be up there; but try not to make noise, sometimes he's asleep." There was no comment about him being in my room from Zelena, I guess she didn't even want to know anymore. Plus, we were in high school, it didn't matter all that much.

Walking up the stairs I had a really strong feeling that he was in there, probably dozing, not unusual.

I opened the door to find him lying out on my bed; he opened his eyes and sat up, a pleasant smile, though a small one, appeared on his gorgeous face.

"Wynter, I've been waiting for you-"

Zelena stepped from behind me, looking around like she was confused. I turned back to my bed to introduce them, but all I could see and think about after then was on the fact that it was empty.

The window a few feet away was open, letting the outside rain in and apparently Chase out.

"Wyn, there isn't anybody here, who are you talking to?" Zelena asked.

"He was just right there! Didn't you see him? He jumped out the window, I guess-" my voice trailed off. She hadn't seen him; all she saw was her best friend talking to an empty room. And that meant that Chase was out there in the pouring rain. How had she not seen him? How had he left so fast? More questions, but that didn't matter now. For him to leave like that meant that it had upset him more than I thought it had. Which meant that I had to fix things, preferably sooner rather than later.

"Lena, go home, I'm sorry, but go home I have to go find him! I'll explain later . . . if I can." I started away before she could pull me back, like I thought she would want to.

"But Wynter!" She called after me, but I was already out the window and scrambling down the tree that was growing conveniently next to it. She would leave; she would forgive me, Chase . . . I don't know because I haven't been in a situation like this with him before now. Damn Zelena and her need to meet him.

I got to where Chase was pretty fast, because the only thing I knew for certain about him was that he would be at our secret place. Coming to the lake, I saw Chase ahead of me, soaked, like me, by the rain.

"Chase? Chase. C'mon!" I ran over to him, deciding that talking to his back might be easier right now. He has always been stubborn; the guy would probably just turn his back on me if I talked to his face.

"Chase, what is your *problem*? I'm sorry I didn't ask you, I'm sorry that I didn't listen to you when you said you didn't want to meet Zelena, but I made a choice, I didn't think that you would bolt. Stop being such a drama king." He was pissing me off. It wasn't life or death; he needed to get over himself. Funny how I could love him so much and at the same time want to scream at the things he did.

Those words were left hanging in the air, for Chase to grab, or to leave. He started walking away, but I needed more. The rain poured down on us, I was freezing, and the lack of jacket didn't help. I grabbed feebly onto Chase's jacket and held tight, there was no way I was letting go now.

"Chase. Why are you so hell bent on not meeting Zelena? Do you know her and hate her? You're not shy, we both know that. How come you can know everything about me but you don't want to know my other best friend? Why do you do things like that?" I was mad; he knew it, madder than I've been at him.

"Do things like what, Wynter?" He seemed reluctant to ask.

"Don't give me that, you know exactly what I mean. Not just now, all the time. Why do you refuse to meet Zelena? Why won't you meet me anywhere in public? What, are you embarrassed of me or something? Can't be friends with me in front of other people or something like that? Hell I don't know anything about you, Chase. Why *is* that?"

"You really want answers?" I nodded my head; sure that he could feel the motion against his back. This was ridiculous. But it looked like I was going to get some answers to the questions that I had about him, so maybe it was for the better.

"I want to know why Zelena isn't allowed to see you, why you ran away so fast, where you live, your school, I want to know you Chase. You know me, everything about me. I want to know who you are." It was the truth. Because I had no idea.

"To trust you? Wynter, is that what your asking? It sounds like it. However I don't want to condemn you to my secrets, I don't want you to have to deal with the horror I deal with everyday."

"Chase, c'mon. It can't be that bad, really. I want to know, I want to help you, Chase. Do your parents hit you? Were you hurt as a child? Do you live somewhere you think is embarrassing? Even if it's scary, if it's weird, I don't care. Whatever it is it'll be easier to tell me rather than annoy me with doing things like this. I want to be there for you like you have been for me." I hugged him, never planning to let my arms drop; because this was clearly something deeper than not wanting to meet a new person. This seemed to be a trust thing. And if he had trust issues, I wasn't going to leave him now. That would just make it a whole lot worse.

"I don't want you in my world, it's dark, it's scary to humans like you. Once you know about one of my kind, about me, your eyes will be opened to the rest of . . . us."

"Trust me, Chase, I can help you." I wrapped my brain around what he had just said, whispering his words out loud, making sure that I had heard them correctly.

Humans like you? My kind? What the hell is he talking about?

It took him three long moments to turn around, I could detect sadness written across his face, unwillingness, and then something else, a smug look maybe? But that twittered by so fast I decided that it must have been just rain in my eyes.

He raised my face to look at him, and widened his mouth, a half smile, and half snarl. What I saw made me realize why he never really let me see him smile. There were four razor sharp teeth, two on the top and two on the bottom, in his mouth. I felt my jaw drop slightly and I turned to look into his eyes.

Everything was becoming clear, everything that didn't make sense before just clicked into place with that one look he gave me.

"Wynter."

I leaned into him, shaking, due to the cold that was settling really deep in my bones, or what I knew he was going to say next, I don't know.

"I'm a mythical creature, I'm an abomination, I'm evil. And you know this because you can tell what I really am now." He grabbed my cheeks and looked at me so intensely I didn't feel alive, "I'm a vampire."

It explained everything. With the icy rain from the storm, the shock of finding my best friend, the boy I love, was a creature I thought could never exist, and the brain overload, I dropped like a fly. That's right, of course. I fainted.

4

Sick for You

The first bite, it can't get worse,
Now you understand the curse.
I can't love you, never will,
If you love me I will kill.
-Nicole Evans

Coming to, I saw how dark it was around me, dark, not with night, but with clouds. There was a heavy lining of thunderclouds left over from the storm from before. When was that? Yesterday? A few hours ago? I don't have a clue. I looked around to get my bearings and saw that I was in my room. How I got here? No idea. Last thing that I remember was that Chase about to tell me something important, oh what was it? Right on the tip of my mind I went over all that happened last night multiple times to see if that would jog my memory, it didn't.

I moaned and turned over in bed, I felt like I had a hangover. My head was throbbing and I just felt like crap.

Must have been from running around in the rain, you dumb-ass, I told myself.

Something twinkled on the edge of my memory, it was what Chase had said, concentrating real hard. I sat up in bed and griped either side of my temples with each hand.

"You stupid girl!" I said to myself, "It was important, c'mon!" I tried shaking my head back and forth, which only made the pain worse. Then I opened my eyes that were previously squeezed shut to see I was in my pajamas.

"Worry about that later, Chase probably just-" *Helped me out of my wet clothes.* I finished in my head. I took a deep breath and felt my chest. Good, I was still wearing my bra.

He wouldn't take advantage of me that way anyways, I can trust him, but what did he say to me?

It was important! Why couldn't I remember?!

Vampire.

I jumped to my feet and tore on the shoes, which had been on the ground next to the bed, in record time.

"Chase you idiot! You can't just leave me here after telling me something like that!" I was talking to myself angrily, perfect. I was half way out the window, ready to go find him, when a voice surprised me from a corner in my room:

"I didn't."

I whipped my head around and fell into a crouch, preparing to beat the hell out of whomever it was in my room without me knowing it.

"Chase!" I immediately stood up, kicked my shoes off, and ran over to him, enveloping as much of his torso as I could into my arms. He was still damp, that meant he probably had this rotten cold too, or was soon going to.

"Why are you still wet? You're gonna catch your death! Come here stupid, get outta that wet stuff." I let him go, and realized what I had just said. I asked him to get out of his clothes, oh great was I gonna get it.

But he just started taking his shirt off, making no eye contact with me and not questioning what I had just told him to do, thank God.

I needed something to occupy my hands and eyes so while he was doing that I looked around for anything of mine that would fit him. Unfortunately unless he wanted to wear black ripped skinnies, he was out of luck.

"Will a blanket do while I'm drying your-" I turned around to see him without a shirt or pants on, covered only by his boxers, standing directly in front of me. He reached around my side, almost touching me but not quite, to grab the confronter off of my bed.

"Yes, this will do fine." So cold.

"Y-es u-m—ye-ah dry-yer, me cloth-es, bye." I muttered incoherently to him, grabbed the pile of wet clothes from off of the floor, and ran downstairs to dry them. Trying to cool my red face off coming back upstairs I took deep breaths.

I guess the heavy breathing on top of my cold and running up and down stairs was too much for me. 'Cause eventually I saw black dots in front of my face and had to lean against the wall for support. Slowly I started sinking down the wall to sit on the stairs, waiting for the dizziness to pass.

Out of the corner of my eye I thought I saw someone coming, but that was ridiculous and passed it off as nothing. It was only when I heard a voice that I actually realized Chase had found me sitting on the stairs.

"Idiot. You're more sick than me, you can't go running up and down stairs like that, it's only going to get worse."

"Well excuse me if I wasn't aware of that Mr. Know-It-All." I said in between slow easy breaths, trying to clear me head, it wasn't the first time it's happened, in fact I had a problem with fainting, and I knew how to care for it.

"You know it happens a lot when I stand too fast, just gimmie a sec." I put my head down, what I normally did.

Suddenly I felt strong arms around my back and under my legs, and it took me the time to be lifted into the air before I registered that Chase was carrying me up the rest of the stairs in to my room.

"Hey! Hey put me down! I'm gonna freaking break you Chase! Your sick too!" I yelled in his ear, he only held me away from his body and moved his head back away from me as well. Then I saw his lack of clothing and started fighting to be let free.

"Awh come *on*! You can't get worse sick!"

"That sentence didn't make sense Wynter." So distant.

"Whatever! Just let me down!" I kicked my way out of his arms, or tried to at least, I didn't want him to know how heavy I was. He was probably straining under the weight anyway. But when I looked up at his face he didn't look strained in the least, so I stopped struggling. My reward was being held closer to his bare chest, so worth it. I crossed my arms anyway, I could at least look angry to be held like this.

"You know," I said as he set me down onto my bed and sat next to me, "You should have taken care of yourself first, I don't want you sick any more than you want me sick."

Chase looked torn between wanting to talk and wanting me to shut up so that he didn't have to.

"My kind is more stable compared to yours."

"Your kind?" I questioned, "What do you mean-oh, that your kind." I looked up to make sure that I didn't just insult him with forgetting. I guess I had.

A disgusted look passed over his face and he stared down at me, fury written all over him.

"How could you forget what I am?" He spat out.

"Look, sorry Chase I just wasn't thinking, I'm sorry if I insulted you-"

"Insulted?" He interrupted me and the fury died down from his face, only a hint of disgust was left there, but whether it was towards him, or me I didn't know.

"It's surprising that you're able to forget that so quickly. I just told you and you seem to already be over it. That's not normal Wynter, it's weird enough that you're not running away terrified, even weirder that you let me hold you, but this?"

His disgust was battling with another emotion, I think it was confusion.

"I *was* scared though. I fainted." I felt terrible about that, but it was just such a shock I guess I couldn't handle it. "Thank you, though. For taking care of me, for putting me in dry clothes," I blushed at that one, and he turned his head away, I think he was doing the same thing, "And for not leaving. I really wish you had taken better care of yourself though."

He tried to explain my fainting, "I believe it was more of the storm and you trying to think again, I keep telling you not to do that, idiot." Warmth in his voice, it was so good to hear.

"Hey, you made me think so it isn't my fault!"

He laughed, and I closed my eyes to enjoy the sound coming from his mouth. Turning back to me once again, he was smiling, and I could see it, my favorite sight in the whole world, the sight that I wanted to preserve forever. I could see the tips of all four of his fangs just peaking out from under and above his lips. To my surprise, they didn't scare me at all.

Realizing what I was looking at, his smile instantly vanished, much to my disappointment. The darkness from the lack of lights being on in my room and outside the window concealed his expression from me this time.

"Chase, it's okay, I'm not scared." I said, crawling over to comfort him, it was mostly the truth anyway, I knew that he couldn't and wouldn't hurt me.

"And that scares me Wynter."

"Why?"

"Because I believe you. You should be scared of me, but you aren't. You should be running away, I keep waiting for you to, but you don't. It's not normal, I would think that you're one yourself if I knew that you couldn't be."

"I always believed in something other than humans. I mean we can't be the only ones here that have really big brains or whatever, can we?"

"I suppose you believe in aliens too, don't you?"

"Duh."

I don't like serious moments, so the little jokes thrown in meant a lot. I knew that Chase was uncomfortable with them as well, not the jokes, the seriousness. He fiddled with the blanket that he had pulled over himself to keep warm, a sure sign that he was feeling this silence like me.

"Well how do you know that?"

"Know what, Wynter?"

"That I'm not a vampire, maybe I'm one in disguise, just waiting to suck your blood!" I said imitating something I'd read in *Dracula*, the book. Apparently that didn't bother him, which now that I think about, could have.

"You can't stay standing for more than five minutes. You'd let your own shadow trip you."

"Well that was mean! I wouldn't let me shadow trip me. She just does it when she knows I'm not paying attention!" He cracked a smile, and I knew that under the circumstances that was pretty good.

"You talk about your shadow in third person." He pointed out.

"She clearly has a mind of her own." I replied back to him.

A light clicked on in my head and something dawned on me that I should have realized before this.

"That's why you always seem so interested in my neck!" I cried out, and then regretted it. I began thinking I should have left that alone, but to my relief, he chuckled.

"Partly. What you humans made up about my kind isn't entirely true, we don't have to bite the neck, it's just easier than being kicked or punched in the face by flailing limbs. But you have an attractive neck so yeah, I like it." It was so simply put but all the same it flustered me.

I blushed, making his smirk his evil little smirk. Then he pulled me closer, his hand on my chin. He was pulling me up and leaning down himself.

This is absolutely it. There's no way to mistake this one. He leaned his head a little to the side, as I did too, I let my eyes close halfway. *Here we go!*

Then, just as our lips were about to make contact I heard the distinctive buzzing noise of my cell phone on the bedside table.

Buzzzzt. Buzzzt. Buzzzt.

The moment was lost and Chase pulled back, I was going to kill whomever texted me.

>> **Whr r u?**<< It was from Zelena . . . still might kill her.

"Who is it?" Chase asked, though he probably already knew.

"Zelena, must be wondering why I'm not in school today after ditching her yesterday." I went to put the phone back but his hand covered mine, stopping it.

"Reply, I don't want her worried about you." I looked at him, wondering if he was just saying that, "Really, go on, I'd want you to do the same for me." I didn't want to point out that he didn't have a cell phone, so I texted her instead.

>> **Home, i'm sick):** << The reply came a few seconds later. She must be in English, it was too easy to text and not get caught in that class.

>> **Rly? r u w chase?** << I looked to him, trying to decide if I should tell her the truth or not.

>> **No, well yeah, but he's just taking care of me.** <<

>> **O, want me 2 hlp?** << I relied her offer to him and he shook his head.

"I got it, besides we probably have more to talk about." He said.

"True." I replied

>> **Thanks but he says it's cool, doesn't want us both out with whatever I have.** <<

>> **Kk, but if u need anything, just say so.** << Zelena really was a nice person.

>> **Thanks, text you later.** <<

>> **Feel better, byee[:<3** <<

>> **Bye (:** <<

It didn't take long for our conversation to end, seeing as though she was in class still, so I put my cell on silent and turned back to him.

"Her shorthand is really confusing," He commented.

"Yeah but the more you read it the easier it gets to understand. I can't bring myself to butcher words like that so I don't." He laughed quickly and softly.

"So I'm sorry about that," I apologized for texting in the middle of our conversation, "She was worried."

"Yeah, I know, it's alright."

"She still wants to meet you, you know."

"She can, now that you understand it's safer I think. I just won't smile for her."

"Fine with me! Then I get to keep it all to myself, no one can see you smile except for me! You will smile for me, won't you Chase?" I looked at him with what I hoped were puppy dog eyes, regardless or if they were or not, it worked.

"Urgh, fine. Just quit with the face," he covered my head with his hand.

"Oh you just say that 'cause it's working!" I pried his fingers from my face and held onto his arm possessively.

"You look like a dying poodle." I stuck my tongue out but I knew in my mind I probably did look like a dying poodle. I jumped from where I was sitting on the bed and tackled him. He dragged me onto his lap and I rested my head by his shoulder.

"Smile for me!" I screeched in his ear. He didn't. I gave up right away, thinking I would be able to get one out of him later.

"Can you tell me more about your kind? Like can you fly? How fast are you? How many humans have you taken blood from?" We both visibly cringed at that one, "Can Zelena even see you? How can I see you? Can you see yourself in a mirror? What about pictures? Where are other vampires?" I would have continued firing off questions to him, but he stopped me with his hand over my mouth, knowing I would go on forever.

"One at a time Wynter! Anyway, we'll talk about this later, right now you need rest or you won't be able to go outside again for a long while." That shut me up since I knew the weather was going to be perfect clouds for at least a day or two, and I didn't want to waste it.

"Ok, but you gotta tell me tomorrow then at least!" I made him promise. He got up and placed me into my bed. I yawned, the sheets looked so inviting.

"Don't worry, we have plenty of time for your questions, which I'm sure are going to be relentless, am I right?"

"But of course!" I said with a grin, but now I needed to sleep. Chase was right, I didn't want to waste the clouds this coming weekend and I was tired anyway. Stupid cold.

I felt myself drifting off to sleep, all while he was touching my face. I couldn't keep my eyes open and knew it was only a matter of time before I drifted off into my dreams, maybe I already had. Probably.

"Thanks Chase." I managed to get out, "I love you." The hand that was soothing my face moved to my hair.

"I know Wynter, now go to sleep."

"Say you love me too Chase." I don't even know if he heard me, I was completely out of it.

"I love you too, Wynter." I smiled, I liked this dream, Chase told me he loved me.

5

Fondly Worshiped

You're my addiction,
You're my drug,
You're my weakness,
A grave I dug.
-Nicole Evans

The days that followed were a blur to me, much to my dismay. The cold that I had developed from the time I spent in the rain started off simple, but escaladed to the full-blown flu. Chase recovered quickly, only took a good nights sleep. Then he stuck with taking care of me, he did the whole time.

Zelena visited a couple of times before Chase made her stop, saying that two people with the flu wasn't going to help anything.

They met. I had to set it up and hold Chase's attention the whole time, so that he wouldn't let his guard down, as he says he does too much around me. It was only for a little while, but Zelena seems to trust him, it's hard to look and be around him without trusting him completely.

I lay in bed, thinking back to the day they met, having nothing else to do.

~ ~ ~ ~ ~

"Just keep looking at me, I'll distract you, and-"

"What if she sees my teeth?"

"Don't worry about that, if you start to let your guard I'll fake that I need your help with something. Anyways were not going to eat and you rarely smile so I don't think that'll be a problem."

We were sitting in my room; rather Chase was sitting on a chair next to my bed, which I had been lying on for the past day or so. It had taken a while but I finally got Chase to agree to meet Zelena, but now he was asking all the "what ifs" he possibly could. Chase laid his face on the covers on my stomach in utter defeat.

"But I don't wanna!" I played with his wavy brown hair, a beautiful shade of dark caramel, while he was reduced to begging not to meet my other best friend. Chase continued mumbling, I wasn't really listening. It went on like this for a few more moments until I heard:

"She's going to find something out and I'll have to leave!" No! I pulled his head up; my eyes were wide and already filled with tears at the thought of him leaving me. I looked at him; he seemed surprised that I reacted. Both of us sat up and I started to cry.

"You can't! Never! I don't care who finds out, you can't leave Chase!" I grabbed his head up in my arms, tackling him from his chair to the floor.

"Shhh, shh it's okay, I'm sorry, I shouldn't have said that, of course I won't leave you Wynter." He said it like he had a secret though. What did that mean? Chase kept trying to calm me down, and eventually I did, but the tear streaks were still there. He was rubbing them away when

the door opened. Zelena walked in to see the two of us on the ground. I looked like I had been crying, I had been, and Chase's hands were on my face. The chair was knocked by the force of my tackle and lay a foot or so away.

"This is absolutely not what I wanted to walk in on." Her coolness at the situation surprised me, but I guess I had prepared her enough to expect something like this. God I prepared them like he was my boyfriend meeting my super religious and strict parents or something. Chase scooped me up in his arms and got up himself, setting me on my feet, all while making sure to keep his back to her.

"Lena! Sorry, I was just . . . actually never mind." She rolled her eyes, knowing that if it was important I would tell her later, if not then she concluded that she probably didn't wanna know.

"Zelena, this is Chase, and Chase, this is Zelena." She hadn't gotten a very good view of Chase, only his back. When he turned around to really meet her she did the same thing I did when I first met him, she gasped.

I could see her take him in, looking him over. I don't know if it was for my sake or just because of his beauty, either way I had to feel a tinge of jealousy. I don't know if beautiful the correct term for guys but it is here, for him, everything about him is beautiful, gorgeous even. And since Zelena was taking the time to look him over, I thought I would too, just for the sake of it.

Chase was muscular, I knew that from him picking me up all the time with no strain, but he wasn't obnoxiously so. His coal eyes seemed to stare straight into your soul, while his wavy brown hair seemed to block you out of him own, seeing as though it covered most of his eyes. Never in my 17 years of life had I seen someone like him, I don't think I ever would again either.

It sounds so plain, so normal, when I describe him. Unfortunately I can't really capture his essence when I speak. But if you just saw him, you would understand. It's like this being that he carries about himself.

"E-hem, nice to meet you?" Chase interrupted our impolite staring by putting his hand out to meet Zelena's, who weakly grabbed it from the air and shook it back.

"Nice to meet you Chase. Um, sorry about that, Wynter has an annoying habit to talk about you but she failed to completely express your looks, I wasn't prepared." Blunt much?

"Zelena!" I hissed at her, turning to look at Chase. He was only half facing me, but I could tell that he had an amused tinkle in his eyes, as well as his signature smirk on those lips.

"Well, well. What else has my little WynWyn said?" His amusement was evident in his voice, I tried to give Zelena a look, but it was promptly ignored.

"Oh God, a lot, it's all she talks about!"

"No it isn't! I talk about a lot of other stuff too!" They both loved this.

"Well she is right, once in a while she talks about the homework she hasn't done . . . because she was with you, then it's back to talking about something to do with what you guys did recently." I was surely dying of humiliation, but not enough to realize that Chase's smirk was growing. I knew it was near impossible not to smile near Zelena, but I expected not to have to worry about it with Chase.

"Oh shit!" I pretended to lean too far forward trying to get Zelena to shut up and fell out of the bed. Chase stopped me from hitting myself too hard, as I knew that he would. Shooting him a look, realization crossed his face and he nodded, just enough for me to see.

From then on the three of us stuck to the topics that would both amuse us but at the same time keep Chase from showing much other than a slight upturn on his lips. As the conversation began to slow down I began to find it harder and harder to keep my eyes open.

"Well it looks like Wynter should be going to sleep now, so I'm going to ask you to leave, if that's alright." Chase motioned to the door for Zelena's exit.

"Oh, yeah, alright, I should be going anyways. Well it was nice to meet you Chase, take care of Wyn for me, you hear?"

"Will do, you have nothing to worry about." Zelena walked over to me, placing one hand on my hair, another beside my head; she bent down and whispered into my ear.

"If you need anything at all, I'm just a call away, love you Wynter, and get well soon." I barely mumbled a response, but knew that she knew I was saying thanks.

She left and I fell fast asleep, knowing that the danger of Chase being found out was gone for the time being.

~ ~ ~ ~ ~

Over the days that followed Chase took care of me, only leaving the house a few times for medicine, food, and a change of clothes for himself. Zelena came to visit and watch me when he left.

It was Sunday night when I got fed up with lying around doing nothing, I had started feeling fine by Saturday but Chase insisted that I stay in bed an extra day. I hadn't been allowed to ask him any of my burning questions about vampires; apparently it would 'cause too much stress and make me relapse. Yeah, okay, the liar. He said the first day that when I woke up that I could ask him stuff. Stupid Chase.

Whatever, he promised, I'm fine now, so there's no excuse for him not to. I silently climbed out of bed, if he caught me going downstairs now I'd just be thrown back to sleep more.

Stealthy, Wynter! I made it down to the kitchen, where Chase was, before he knew I was out of bed.

"Back up Wynter c'mon, you wanna go to school tomorrow don't you?" I sat down at the kitchen table; he did the same thing on the other side.

"Not really, and anyways you're not my mom Chase, stop acting like that it's boring!" I wined, silently begging him to not make me go back upstairs.

"Yeah, yeah fine whatever."

"You said you'd tell me about your kind, sooo begin! Right now! Onward!"

"For real? Wynter . . . you just got better." He was grabbing at nothing, I so won.

"No, actually I got better a while ago but you're trying to buy time. I'm 17 not 12, I won't fall for that now *start* damn you!"

"Alright well I promised I guess." The look I was directing in his general direction made him back down.

"What you wanna know?"

"How old are you?"

"19, like I've always said I was." *19?*

"Aren't you guys supposed to be like a thousand and be able to live forever?" Chase sighed; I guess it was a typical human question he had been expecting. He leaned back onto the two hind legs of his chair, surveying the kitchen area before continuing.

"Ok before I answer anything else, I'm going to tell you all the bull that humans fed each other about vampires." I nodded in response, signaling for him to go on.

"We can't live forever-"

"Why not?" I got a warning look not to even start interrupting.

"We can't live forever because we can't. Why can't human's life forever? Because they can't, I don't have a real explanation for that. Our life spans are much longer than humans are though, roughly 200 years, if nothing goes wrong, though most stop aging at 20 to 25 or so. Furthermore, before you even ask, garlic doesn't kill us, nor does the sun." I began to open my mouth to ask why but his eyes whipped to mine so fast I kept it shut and let him continue.

"Our senses are much stronger than yours, so the smell of garlic bothers us, but many strong smells do. Our eyes are equipped mostly for the dark, so bright sunlight irritates them, that's why the majority of us hang out after the sun sets, or on foggy days." That explained why he likes my favorite weather so much.

"I can see myself and you can see me in mirrors, pictures come out too. Really, I don't know where you guys come up with all this shit. We can't turn into bats, that's the most annoying one, who in God's name thought of that one??" He was talking more to himself than me with that last one.

He spent a second trying to think, "That's all that comes to mind that would irritate me if you asked." I immediately began interrogating him.

"Whose blood have you drank, do they die? How does that all work? Oh, oh do they turn into vampires too?!" I got real excited about the last one.

"Seems I forgot to mention that," Chase rubbed his temples, looked like he was trying to think, "We can turn humans into vampires, that much is true."

"Really? By sucking their-"

"However—not just by sucking their blood." I was confused. "Pardon a few rogue vampires or an extremely thirsty one, we don't drain our victim to death. We'll take a little from each person that we choose, so that they live. Depending on choice, a vampire can either erase the memory of their victim after the attack, or make it so that they are unconscious before."

"How?"

"Not so sure on that one, it's just something we can do, it comes naturally to us, like breathing. Look into the victims eye's, will it, and it's done." I thought on this for a while, how I wouldn't mind being mesmerized by Chase's eyes, though I am everyday anyways.

"So how can a human be turned into a vampire?" His eyes sparkled both with knowledge as well as a gleam of triumph, though I don't know why.

"Well, when sucking blood, that is the vampires only concern, to be filled until the next time. But when an attachment is formed between a human and a vampire, a strong attachment like one of love, the human's blood becomes very incredibly appealing to said vampire, hundreds of times more appealing to them than any other person."

"Ok, so, for example, if a human falls in love with a vampire, or the other way around?" I asked, blushing at the use of the word love around him.

"No, the feeling has to be mutual to some extent. Although there have been some cases that I've heard of where either the human or vamp are so in love with the other that it makes up for the other not having that feeling, that is rare though."

"So what happens after the bond is formed?"

"There are two choices that the vamp can make. One is to make the human into a vampire themselves. This happens by biting a human and forcing venom into their bloodstream, instead of sucking blood out. Then normally those two stay together until death, like a marriage, or what marriages are supposed to be like anyways."

"And what's the other choice?" The triumph shimmered even brighter in his eyes, the corners of his mouth twisted up ever so slightly.

He must really like this aspect of his life or something, though I have to say that look is a little . . . creepy.

"The other option is to make the human either a blood bride or groom, depending on the sex." He was trying to make me uncomfortable; it was working, evil vampire. He didn't go on, just stared at the ceiling; I knew he wanted me to ask.

"Ok, I give, what's a blood bride." I finally questioned him.

"I'm glad you asked," I rolled my eyes, "That's when a vampire pushes venom into a human, enough to sustain it to keep it living for as long as the vampire, but not enough to completely change them or give any powers, as many call them. Generally they stay together like a couple as well, but instead of being equals the human helps their partner stay alive all that time." It took me a few minutes to digest all of that; I had to think it over a few times.

To be a vampire, have powers, and live with the one they love for 200 years. Or, to service the vampire one loves with blood for 200 years, to sustain them no matter what. The first sounds more . . . bearable, but the second one makes the new half-bread I guess, useful. Tough choice.

"What are the powers that you're talking about?"

"It's not really powers, most of them are human traits as well, we just do everything your kind can do about 1000 times better."

"For example . . ." This was interesting.

"Running and jumping, we can do both for very long amounts of time, and very fast. This is to ensure that no prey escapes."

"Makes sense I guess, no flying?"

"Nope. We don't turn into bats either, like I just said a minute ago, and wooden stakes aren't a sure-kill. We have normal skin, like a human. So if you shoot us or stab us in the heart with anything, we'll die." I laughed, which I think was what he meant to accomplish.

"You can feel pain though, and get sick." It wasn't a question so much as it was a statement, I knew this from previous incidents.

"We can get sick, but it takes very little time to get better, and we can get hurt, it just won't hurt as much and won't do as much damage."

I seemed to run out of questions for a while and ended up making tea for myself, coffee for Chase. Turns out that they can eat and drink our food, it's just more for pleasure than filling up. Upon questioning it Chase said that to them blood tasted better but once could survive for some time on normal food.

"Where do you go to school?" Not a question about vampires, not even vaguely related, but that had always bothered me.

"I don't." My raised eyebrow probed him further for questions. "I mostly just stay here, at your house, or sort of hang around places."

"So you have no education then? What about a job or college or something?"

"I don't need a job and as for education, I know enough to live, that's how vampires live and how humans used to live. Your kind used to just learn enough to live and were okay; now you all feel the need to learn everything and the world is suffering in a lot of ways thanks to it."

"So you just stay here or talk around? Well I guess that would explain the shadow following me to and from school, Chase you're a creeper!" I accused him, pointing my finger.

"What are you talking about? When? I don't do that . . . often, not lately anyway."

"Oh, maybe it's my imagination, been going on for a month or so though." Chase didn't look happy about that, but personally I passed it off as nothing. Being pretty sure that I was crazy anyway, this was probably just a symptom of it.

The two of us, Chase and I, talked for the rest of the day, taking a walk and eating lunch in between discussions. He told me how when Zelena was watching me he was really hunting, as I liked to call it. I told him that I was really just sitting there doing nothing, pretty deceptive of me. But throughout the time we spent together, and mainly outside, I couldn't help but notice a flash of something around every few corners, or Chase's constant watch in front of us and behind us.

There was a continual eerie feeling surrounding us of being watched, I'm sure we both noticed it, although neither of us commented on it. Besides everything was safe as long as I was by Chase's side.

Of course it was.

6

Splatter my Blood

Where does one go, when all is gone?
When everything known, just vanishes in white.
Well, inside ones self, but of course.
Retreat back to your inner core and hibernate.
-Nicole Evans

At first, knowing about Chase and his way of life didn't seem to affect me much at all. He drank blood for survival. Okay, well I eat for survival. But something about it just seemed so *wrong* and I burned up with some sort of feeling that wasn't comfortable, not at all. It took my daydreaming, Chase being the object of these daydreams of course, and the observing of my classmates to realize just why I didn't like his feeding habits.

Most girls, or normal people in general, would be disgusted from the get go. But I didn't become disgusted with animals that ate raw meat, so I shouldn't be with him, either.

My math class was in the process of discussing something like parabolas; as usual I wasn't paying attention, rather looking around at what my classmates were doing. One kid with obnoxiously red hair was zip tying another kid's backpack together, after he had turned it inside out. Some girls were discussing chickens and fruitcakes, which was actually normal for them. Then there were the two girls in the center of the room, pretending to take notes but were really playing monopoly on their iPod Touches, which they did just about every day.

One of the girls, the one with brown hair, I think her name was Michelle? I don't know, as I've said, I never pay attention. Well she was taking breaks every few minutes from her game to draw some really fat old person in a sweater or a kid with red hair. Whispers of the word gingers, followed by giggling, came from their seats every few minutes. The two were very, very loud so I couldn't help but overhear their annoying conversation, which actually pinpointed my problem with Chase drinking blood.

"So I was hanging out with Steve yesterday." Brownie started.

"Well yeah, duh, he *is* your boyfriend after all." Her friend with wavy blonde hair replied.

"Shut up, anywho I was talking to him and then he kept texting someone and I was like 'who are you texting?' and he was like 'no one' so I kept asking and it turns out that he was texting some girl I didn't know." Brownie gave Frizzy a look, a sad one I presume, but I couldn't see it so well, only hear.

"Oh, well was he like, um, saying thing that he probably shouldn't or something, like hitting on her?" I thought her question was kind of blunt and unfeeling, but she never seemed to have barriers when she talked.

"No but it's like, the action may be innocent and he claims he had to, for homework I guess, but I mean he's my boyfriend and I should help him, not someone else. Especially another girl." The rest of their conversation died out before it hit my ears. That was *exactly* what it was to me!

Sure, Chase needs to get blood, that's understandable, but what if his victim was a girl? A stake of horror pierced through my heart, as I imagined the actions that have probably happened and most likely will happen again.

Chase stalking a girl, probably a pretty one just for the sake of it, then meeting her on the street or in a field, wherever they could be alone. Coming up to her, more than likely seducing her with his walk and just plainly himself, then pressing his perfect lips to her neck, like he had to me. I imagined the seductive pleasure of having him bite into my neck, her neck, whoever's neck. Then the look of satisfaction that would surely follow from his drinking. Clenching my fists I stood up and slammed my hands down on the desk.

"Ms. Hayes! What's going on? Is there a problem?" My teacher, Mrs. Scingy, asked me in a stern voice.

"Mrs. Factor!" Fruitcake girl calls her that; don't ask why, "I think she-"

"I can talk myself, thank you." I replied in a frosty manor. Fruitcake stopped talking, contently humming and drawing chickens on her notebook.

"I need to go to the bathroom." Taking my bag and books I started to leave the room, not really waiting for permission. I have anger management problems; I don't want to deal with them. Any little thing can set me off and now I was ready to kill somebody.

"Wynter." I turned around to face her, this better be important, "Did I say you could leave?" Her calm tone just made me angrier. I was ready to punch the wall, as I have before in a class of hers, but refrained myself. Instead I choose to explain with something she couldn't respond to.

"I'm sorry, but at the moment I'm experiencing severe cramps because I guess it's just that time of month for me; so I'm just going to go to the nurse to get some nice meds then go to the bathroom to shove a tampon right up my-"

"That's quite enough. Go." Mrs. Scingy cut me off, battling between a disgusted and angry look, the class was cracking up.

"Why thank you Mrs. Scingy," I said in my best sugar sweet voice. Walking out of the classroom I headed to my locker. Upon arriving there I threw everything in and grabbed what I would need for the homework I wouldn't end up doing. Threw open the side door out of school, then raced home as fast as I could.

"Stupid Chase, taking blood from girls he doesn't know." *He did need it, it's not like he slept with them or something.* I argued with myself, "Doesn't matter, he could have just asked me!" *Really? How? 'Oh hi Wynter, how are you doing today? Nice weather we're having, isn't it? Oh and can I drink your blood, I'm a vampire by the way.'* "No! Just . . . I may be a little jealous of them, getting to help Chase like that. *I wanna be the only girl to help him.*" I talked to myself often, it scares people away, and they think I'm crazy, which is probably true.

Continuing home I realized that I couldn't take my anger out on him, it wouldn't be fair, so I'd do what I do in any other case: I'd hit a tree. I unlocked my front door after I had arrived and pitched my school stuff on the living room floor, then directed myself to the backdoor which lead to the woods.

I had a favorite punching tree, which was often used, despite the attempt to control my temper. It used to be worse when I got made fun of. I used to care what people thought and said, about my parents leaving me, about my looks; that sort of thing. It's a creative outlet in my opinion. I walked right up to it and without breaking stride smashed my fist into the side of it. A bird flew out of the tree, disturbed by the noise.

"God I hate girls. I hate them!" I grunted and lifted my other fist to release my fury. Even if a feeling doesn't start off as fury, it normally ends up that way for me. If I'm mad, I get angry, obviously, if I'm jealous I get angry, if I'm sad I get angry and such like that. The tree has quite a few nice marks in it.

I continued using both of my fists to put as many dents into the tree as possible, little by little I started to feel better and think clearer. *It wasn't their fault.* Hit. *Chase really did choose them, they didn't volunteer.* Hit. *It's not his fault either he was just hungry.* Hit. *I suppose I shouldn't be mad, I'll just get him to drink from me from now on!* Hit. *If he lets me that is . . .* hit.

The adrenaline had made me forget about the pain in my fists, as always, but now that I felt better, a whole lot better, the pain surged through my fists and fingertips.

"Christ that *hurts*!" I yelped, dancing in a circle while trying to hold my now bloody hands without hurting them any more. "God, Wynter, you're so stupid! You've got to remember that it'll hurt after! Idiot."

"Wynter, what the hell!" A blur of black sped from deeper in the woods to where I was standing, a dizzying motion. "What the hell is this?" The voice, which was Chase obviously, asked while tenderly holding my hands.

"What does it look like? I hit a tree!" I huffed at him, all while still doing my little jig, trying to distract myself from the now dulling pain.

"Yes, I can see that, but why? Never mind, lets get you bandaged up." He began to go and pick me up but I slithered out of his reach.

"It's no problem, I've done it before, and it looks a lot worse than it really is, trust me. It's actually just the first layer of skin, no problem at all." I blathered, my dance now stopped since the pain has reduced to a throbbing.

"Get it bandaged anyway, you'll get an infection." Chase said icily and pointed to the front door.

"Jeez what's your problem?" I asked, as we walked into the bathroom where I kept the medical bandages and stuff, "They're not even your hands." I guess my bad mood wasn't entirely controlled, he tends to put me in a pissy one every once in a while.

"Not even my hands? Wynter, yeah sure they're not *my* hands their *your* hands! You have to learn to take care of yourself!" He lectured me. I pointedly ignored him while I was applying the ointment, so he shut up.

"Do you need any help?" Chase questioned, seeing as though I was having trouble wrapping one hand with the other already bandaged.

"No, I'm doing quite fine on my own, thanks." I tried to save dignity. A few moments of unsuccessful bandaging later I turned to him and shyly held out my un-bandaged hand. Chase rolled his eyed at my child-like behavior but a small smirk played at his lips. I jumped up on the counter so that he could get to my hands easier.

"So care to explain to me why you were hitting a tree in the first place?"

"No, not really."

"Wynter." A warning tone, I knew I would lose this battle but I might as well delay it for a little longer.

"It's not important, school just had me frustrated."

"That's not true and we both know it, you have to actually pay attention and care to have something frustrate you." I looked down sheepishly; my lack of enthusiasm in school was evident.

"I was just thinking is all."

"About . . ." He led me; I knew it would only end up with me telling him anyways so I just let it out.

"You drink blood from other girls, right? I mean of course you do. And you never have from me but I would let you easily, since I won't be turned, and I got jealous. Yeah I'm telling you outright that I'm jealous. I just wondered if it would be easier for you to drink from me since I'm always here and stuff. I wouldn't mind at all! Truthfully, I just don't want you to . . . um, I don't like thinking of you with other girls." I said the last part meekly, partly hiding my intense blush behind black ringlets.

"Oh." I peaked from behind my wall of hair to look at his face, which showed a mix of three emotions. Confusion, lust (I think), and satisfaction; as if I were following along a nice road he set that leads to a trap. The satisfaction dispersed which left only confusion and lust.

"You would let me bite you?" He said leaning in closer to me. Me sitting on the sink's counter meant that I couldn't do much but back up against the mirror or stand my ground. I knew any amount of hesitation would only result in his immediate back off; he wouldn't push me for this.

"Absolutely." He must have seen the unwavering look I had set upon my face, for he tilted my head to the right the slightest bit, moving my hair and revealing my blush in the process. He stood there, in close proximity to me, unmoving for the most part, save his hand, which was stroking my neck, as if contemplating his next move.

He leaned down and whispered in to my ear.

"You would let me bite you." A statement he followed up by pressing his lips to my neck. Simply pressed there. The movement was not followed by a bite or even a kiss.

"Yes." Came my one-worded breathless reply.

He moved his mouth away from my neck just enough to answer with, "Ah, I see."

I felt his teeth graze against my neck, and felt a warm trickle of blood flow from it. *That explains the paper cut I had on my neck from last time.* I thought to myself. The feeling sent shivers up and down my spine. I gripped the edge of the counter, anticipating more. Slowly

I felt his warm tongue lick up the blood droplet and then he pulled away.

Confusion flittered across my face; I could tell because staring into his eyes I could see myself.

"Unfortunately I just went hunting not too long ago, and am not hungry at the moment." A sigh escaped my lips. "Though I may have to take you up on your offer on a later date." I felt my eyes light up and looked up at his tall figure. I was still unhappy that I didn't have the pleasure of being graced with a bite, and Chase knew that. He was silently laughing at me. But he must have seen that look on my face because the next action astonished me.

"This will have to do, for now." Then he bent down and slowly gave me a light kiss on the lips.

7

Music is Passion

Hold your tongue and speak no more,
Lie's little words are such a bore.
To hear and believe, feed them to me,
Fast or slow, they flow so free.
-Nicole Evans

I wanted him to bite me right this second, but was told that it would be a few more days before he hungered again. For blood anyways. The statement brought up more questions that I wanted to ask, and Chase complied to answer them, under one condition.

He wanted me to go to school for the rest of the week without skipping any classes or leaving in the middle of the day.

It seemed impossible for any senior, especially me, who was known to leave all the time. But nevertheless I wanted to know as much about everything in a vampire's life so I tried wining about it for him to ease up.

"Why do you even want me to stay in school? Don't you like hanging out with me?" I looked down dejectedly, trying to make him change his mind.

"Don't start the faces with me, Wynter." Chase scolded, pulling me into his lap and playing with my hair. "You're not going to change my mind, if you want to know anything ever again, you'll go." We were sitting in my room; it was sunny outside so we didn't want to go outside where we normally would be at this time.

"But why?" I asked, irritated, pulling my hair from him, "Why now? You've never wanted me to go before, well at least you've never cared before! I really, really don't wanna!" I was overreacting, since it was Wednesday that would only leave two days, but it seemed like a long time to someone like me.

"Just do it." Chase said demandingly, pulling my hair back into his hands. "Besides, you know, this Saturday," leaning down he whispered the last part, "I may become hungry again, Wynter." His breath tickled the inside of my ear.

"But if I . . . okay here's a deal." His silence urged me to continue, "Tell me all that I want to know now and I'll give you a promise not to skip anything tomorrow or Friday, I'll even stay after to serve my detentions."

"You can serve all of your detentions in two days?"

"Okay well not all of them, but four at least. They do them in the morning and after school so I'll go early and stay late."

He pondered this a little while, twirling the ends of my hair at the same time. Finally he proposed a counter agreement.

"You do all that, I'll tell you and then you do me a favor that will suit both of us."

"Ok, and what's that?" He pulled my hair back, exposing my ear.

"Keep your promise about letting me bite you." He said seductively and nibbled on my ear with his fangs lightly as he pulled away.

I shivered with unadulterated delight; it was exactly what I was hoping that he would say. No more girls for him but me, I get to help him. I get to be held by him, held close I hoped, and feel his fangs buried into my neck. I nodded at this; turning and looking up to show him that I meant it, showing with my eyes since I didn't trust my voice.

"Good." The smile on his face reached his eyes as well, it made me glad that I was able to make him so happy. I began firing off questions about taking blood and things of that nature.

"What is it like to you?"

"What do you mean?"

"Is it just like eating, filling up, and a normal feeling, or is there something special about it?" Amusement lit in his eyes at my question, as if I was asking a dirty or personal question about him, but he answered it regardless.

"No, not at all, it's defiantly something special." Chase started slowly, choosing his words carefully, "On a random victim there isn't much feeling, but with a willing victim it becomes like a sexual desire." I blushed and he awkwardly looked away.

"Go on," I urged him.

"Wynter are you getting off on this?" He joked.

"*Chase*! What the hell?!" Such a boy. All he could think of was getting off on something . . . but then again I did ask the question.

"Well it's just, that's the only way I can explain it." He laughed, "The actual drinking only takes about a minute or two, depending on how much is being taken and how fast or slow the vampire is drinking."

"What happens if you, well not you, but you know what I mean; drink all the blood in a human?" This was another question that had been taking space up in my mind.

"Well they just die. Nothing to it, really." Simple, they die. New questions didn't arise from that answer until I blurted one out without thinking.

I spoke softly, I could barley hear my own voice, "Have you killed anyone?" He looked away. I hoped the answer was no, and that it didn't offend him. What kind of question was that? God, Wynter, you don't just ask somebody if they have killed another person. Why am I so stupid? I never think before I say things.

"I was expecting that question. Let me put it this way: I haven't killed anyone by draining him or her, and I have never killed anyone who was innocent. I've only ever killed another vampire." That answer wasn't much better in reality.

It shocked me, but I didn't move from his grasp, which had tightened to stop me even if I wanted to. Chase cared about my feelings, but if I wanted something or to know something, he didn't stop me or give me the nice version of a story. I think he believed that if I really wanted to know that I should know everything, not a bridged story or something safe. The world isn't nice, nor is it safe. I consider this all right; it was fair reasoning. In my opinion this could be partly the reason I took the news of him being a vampire relatively well. He didn't hint at it, just told me everything at once. That's much better than me trying to guess at it.

"Don't be frightened, it was for the better." He didn't look like he wanted to talk about it, so I would save those newly thought questions for later.

A few comfortable minutes passed before I asked the question that was really on my mind, I think that Chase was waiting for it.

"How does it feel for humans, like, um, me?" I asked shyly, playing with my fingers, something I did when I was nervous, which wasn't normally often but happened a lot with him.

"How does what feel?" The glimmer in his eyes told me that he was teasing, I sent him my best glare, which only made him laugh but he went on anyway, "I don't know first hand 'cause I'm not a human, but I've heard stories. I've heard lots of stories; most of them were about blood brides, most likely because those are the ones that remember. The girls I know that become blood brides say that they love it. They seem like addicts to me, but there isn't anything bad about that."

"How are they addicts?"

"From what I hear when a human is being bitten the feeling releases great amounts of endorphins, making it a very . . . hot experience. So in other words, if these things I've been told are accurate it will be just about equally pleasurable for the both of us." I looked down and felt my neck heating up, which he could clearly see from where my hair was being pulled. When he said addicts he probably meant the vampire blood-sucking equivalent of sex addicts. Which was awkward, but at the same time, I was glad it wouldn't hurt. I would have gone through with it even if it had but having it feel good was way better.

He was smirking; I knew it, I think over time I had developed a sense to realizing just when he was smirking at me.

"So, now what?" I asked in an attempt to change the conversation, I had my answer there was no reason for me to continue being mocked by him, "Could you tell me why you're making me go to school?" He sighed, but I knew I would get my answer, lately I have been and without much of a struggle.

"After you told me about the feeling of being followed to school I have too noticed a similar feeling when we are outside together or when I am alone. It's probably nothing, I can't sense a human anywhere near us, but I want to take that time to check it out, just in case."

"You can sense if someone is around you?" That was something I didn't expect.

"Most people get that creepy feeling, you're just buried in your music or trying to think. My senses aren't good enough to like pinpoint them or even say for sure that they're there."

"You said a human though," I continued, "Could it be another . . ." My voice trailed off.

"Yeah, I suppose so, which is what I'm worried about. Other vampires are harder to sense in general. It's not impossible, just harder. We tend to be quieter and sneakier than your average human walking about. If a vamp is looking out for another then it's easy to know if one is getting close, but just that, not like if they pose a threat or anything."

"So why do I have to be in school while you're checking all this out? Why can't I just stay at home, or help you?"

"I tend to lose trains of thought and let my guard down when you're around so I want you in school so I can concentrate, and because I want you safe during this time."

"Safe? Are vampires bad with one another? Territorial or something?"

"No, no more than humans, special cases exist where vampires don't get along, but if a human were following you around without making their presence known, would you feel weirded out?" I nodded, that would be quite creepy, and I could see where he was coming from.

"It may be nothing, just us, mostly me, being paranoid," I smiled sheepishly when he said this. I was really paranoid, though I was glad he had included himself on that analogy, "But just to be safe, do me this favor, alright?" I agreed and he picked me up so he, in turn, could stand. I walked to bed and crawled in; he leaned over and gave me a goodnight kiss on the forehead, something he just started doing.

"Will you stay?" I grabbed his hand, as he was walking away from the bed.

"I wasn't planning on leaving, now that you know what I am I have no reason to pretend to go home and sleep." I'm happy with that.

"Mm, oh yeah, I know. My little friend." I snuggled into bed, smiling. He was pretty thoughtful when it all comes down to it.

"I wouldn't call me little, but I am your friend so I'll let it go." He sat on the end of the bed, staring off into nothing.

"Will you be here in the morning?" I asked, my voice slightly muffled by sleep.

"No, most likely not, but remember Wynter, school."

"Yeah, yeah, okay." I drifted off into a dreamless night.

Stupid asshole making me go to school.

~~~~~

The next morning it was hard to get up, knowing that I wouldn't be able to come home until school ended. Regardless of that, I took a shower and got dressed on time, makeup and everything. I grabbed my books and started out the door when I saw a note next to some pop tarts. I knew it was Chase, I mean who else would it be?

> Wynter-
>
> You don't eat enough in the mornings, it's gonna be hard to concentrate if you don't. Heat some of these up before you go, and take them with you on the bus or something. I'll know if you ate them or not. Have a nice long day at school, sucker.
>
> -Chase

Wow, Chase, nice. *I wonder if calling me a sucker was on purpose or just a slip of the tongue?* Regardless. I heated up two of the completely unhealthy, yet extremely delicious, sugar bars and headed out the door to catch the bus. I was eating them on my way down the road and

switching around songs on my iPod. At this pace it took a while to get
to the bus stop since it was at the end of my road, about a quarter mile
away, but it was a pleasant walk.

Waiting in the morning wasn't so bad; the sun hadn't really come
up yet, seeing as though it was only 7 am. It wasn't hot out, but not
too cold to wear a jacket, which was very good.

I fiddled on my iPod, which by the way was my lifeline, and cranked
up "Spring Nicht" by Tokio Hotel. This was the first song that I fell in
love with; it was the first song that I could deem as my favorite. Some
people think I'm too old for the band, I couldn't care less. Their lead
singer's, Bill Kaulitz's, lyrics inspired me to take German, the language
they sang in for the most part. German was the only class I stayed in
almost everyday, I actually really liked it.

It was only about a five-minute wait before I was aboard the bus and
sitting in a puke-green seat. It smelled. I tried to think nasty thoughts
about school, a past time of mine, but the musical bliss of "You Are
So Beautiful," by Escape the Fate, filed my ears and expelled any such
thoughts. The treacherous drive took about 15 minutes more on top of
the two that had already past. Aside from listening to music I just stared
out the window mainly, nobody sat next to me. Zelena wasn't on this bus
and I gave off a 'get the hell away' vibe that kept other students at bay.

Just as I was switching to "Black Label" by Lamb of God a kid I've
never seen before got on the bus. Without looking for other seats he
came to the most obscure seat on the back of the bus, mine.

I raised an eyebrow at him; I could already tell he was interesting.
His outfit consisted of black baggy jeans, a lime green studded belt,
a t-shirt from a band that I didn't recognize, and a leather jacket on
top of that. I was still waiting for some sort of explanation when he
turned around and looked at me. Flipping his straight black hair out
of his face he revealed electric green eyes that pierced directly through
my own blue ones.

"Um, yes?" I kept my cool, but I was churning on the inside. His eyebrow and eyebrow piercing raised, a quizzical look passed over him. I tried to discreetly take him in, while maintaining a slightly pissed look. He had snakebites, studs, an eyebrow piercing, and straight black hair that kept falling in front of his eyes. Chase is hot but this kid was *my* type. All and all, he was quite attractive, but it was his eyes that were just completely extraordinary.

"Wanna explain sitting here? Can you not see that there are plenty of other seats on this thing?" I think I got across the point that I was pretty much a loner.

"Must I?"

"Yes." I liked his attitude.

"My bike just broke down; I needed a ride . . . pretty much anywhere." That would explain the leather jacket I suppose.

"Oh." I turned away, sure he was far from unfortunate looking, quite the opposite, but I had Chase, and so other guys didn't hold my attention for long, if at all. No matter what they looked like.

A few minutes had passed when he took my iPod away to look at the song, nodded at the band and switched it to "Disposable Teens," by Marilyn Manson. He had good taste. Replacing the music player back in my hands we sat and rode in silence for a few passing minutes.

"Have you considered getting some bites?" As of right now I have no hardware, only a bunch in my ears and one in my nose but it still steered people away.

"Yeah, I'm gonna, just haven't gotten off my butt to go get 'em."

"I would if I were you, it would fit." I really need to get on that. Maybe I'll do it myself, I did my ears myself.

"So what's up with your eyes? You got contacts in?" Not exactly a complement, nor an insult, I was merely curious.

"Naw, they're just like that, don't know why."

"Ah okay."

"Does it bother you?" His head was cocked to the side, question written on his face.

"No it's rather striking." Being blunt was one of my many characteristics with people I didn't know very well. I don't have many boundaries.

"Most girls say it looks hot."

"I'm not like most girls." I hated to be compared to 'most girls', or most people in general. It was annoying. He was close to being freaked out at.

"Clearly." Freak out evaded. "You're pretty different Wynter, you know that?" I cracked a smile at this. He wasn't deterred by my coldness or the pissy attitude, seemed to have some sort of taste in style and the fact that he rode a motorcycle didn't hurt.

"As are you." The bus stopped at my school and we followed the other students out the double doors. Standing at the school gates I turned to look at him, "See you around then . . . ?"

"Zeek, my name's Zeek; and yes you most certainly will be seeing me around." I smiled and waved goodbye.

"Until next time, Wynter." I heard him call. I put a hand in the air to signal the same thing. It took me a few steps to think about it. *When did I tell him my name?* I turned around to ask, but by then, Zeek was already gone.

~ ~ ~ ~ ~

"So then I was thinking 'when did I tell this kid me name?' but he had already left." I was explaining my story to Zelena not much later, at our lockers.

"Ok that's interesting and all, but that doesn't explain why you're here in the morning, on time too!"

"Chase is making me stay all day today *and* I have to stay after to serve one of my numerous detentions! Sound unfair or what? I was supposed to come earlier and do a morning detention but whatever," I wined to her.

"I like him even more now!" She laughed and punched me playfully.

I gave her a look, "You don't care if I skip though, I thought."

"I don't but if you don't make them up after school you're gonna get held back and I am absolutely *not* going to have my best friend stay an extra year in high school while I'm in college."

"Blah, blah, blah I'm Zelena I'm nice to my friends blah, blah, blah." I mimicked her in a high voice.

"Shut up and go to class."

"Maybe I will!"

"You have to, sucker!" Was it just me, or was I getting called a sucker more now that I knew of Chase? We went our separate ways, we have a rotating schedule in school so it starts with a different class everyday, and it was confusing. I have English first, I'll say that the English language is terrible, what the hells an intransitive sentence anyways? Beats me. My teacher can't even tell me if I'll use it in the future. I won't.

When I got there I sat against the far wall in the corner, *my* seat. I was very possessive of it. Two others joined me, one listening to her iPod, as I was, and another laughing at a boy in front of the classroom. He looked like he was twelve but apparently was my age, bull.

Our teacher droned on and on about useless stuff and I tried to pay attention, sort of. I took notes that I wouldn't study later and looked ahead, with glazed over eyes. I wasn't the only one, though; the majority of the class was doing the same thing.

After the bell rang and everyone ran for the door I headed out for science, which could have been worse, at least the teacher made sense. We were working with fire today, a lab experiment. It was pretty cool. Some huge kid with a beanie hat pulled almost completely over his eyes and a girl with a really loud voice were in the process of burning the lab equipment. I'm not sure they noticed, they seemed to be dancing or something of that nature. Two girls in matching pink skinny jeans were talking about pulling Fridays, I'm not sure what it meant, but it sounded stupid.

Observing people when they didn't think they were being watched made most of my classes bearable, they really were an amusing bunch. They really made me laugh, or want to at least. I didn't get along with girls that much, too much drama. Zelena was the only exception. She was . . . different. Guys used to talk to me, but I'm so distracted and out there it weirded them out. The cold appearance that I put out was really to keep distance; I loved laughing just as much as the next person, just only with certain people.

My lab partner was gabbing in my ear about something so I ended up helping, having a mildly good time playing with fire.

~~~~~

"Lena, how much longer until the day ends?"

"It's lunch now so only two more hours, okay? Think you can last that long?"

"No I don't think I can." Sitting outside was Zelena's idea, a very bad one I thought, but I complied nonetheless, wanting to make up time I didn't spend with her after school. The courtyard was pretty, I'll admit, but the sun gave off too much heat. At least she let us sit in the shade under a tree.

"So, tell me about yourself, Lena."

"There isn't much to tell, really, I much prefer hearing about you."

"Well talk about *something*, all I do is talk about myself, what have you been up to lately?"

"Mostly writing." Zelena was going to be a writer, or a teacher; whichever came easier to her, though she was amazing at both. I would know. The only reason I'm doing good in school is because she tutors me when I have time.

"What's your book about?" I always questioned her on this, but she'd rather give it to me at the end, when she's finished, in case she messes something up I suppose.

"No matter how much you ask I'm not telling you Wyn."

"Nothing? Anything! C'mon I wanna knowww!" I was being a big baby lately. Oh well, got me what I wanted most of the time. Just 'cause I'm so annoying when I acted like this people just want me to shut the hell up.

"Main characters are Tristan and Serenity. There, you have it."

I tried to get more out of her, but to no results. The two other hours were spent taking useless notes.

Only one more day and I would be rewarded with that bite. I'll admit I was nervous. Not that I would tell Chase that, he wouldn't bite me if he knew that, he's too much of a gentleman. It was nervous anticipation. Because all that I could say in my head was this: *I can't wait.*

8

The Ride of my Life

Fear pours over me,
Dumped unceremoniously.
Icy shock, a lightning thrill,
Pain so deep, it might kill.
-Nicole Evans

Half a day. I was doing all I could to keep busy, in school and out of it. This morning I even gave myself a piercing like that Zeek kid suggested, a lip stud, because it took my mind off of waiting.

Gym was torture, math was torture, English was torture, science was torture, German was the only subject that kept my mind off of the end of the day. I was doing pretty well in it too. Of course that may be because I was copying off of this really smart girl I sat next to. She was pretty useful, and her nails were always fun to look at, done up well. The weather outside was awful, but it was suppose to cloud up by tonight. It was about seventy out, only the air conditioning inside kept me alive.

Chase hasn't come over much the past day, only once for an hour to update me on his search for whomever it was following us. He hasn't found anyone, or had the feeling of being watched, so he's deeming it okay for now. Probably just a passing vampire checking out who else of their kind was around, he had said. I thought it was a hobo, he didn't agree. Since he seemed much more relaxed I didn't tell Chase that I still felt like someone was by me, especially when I was walking to and from the bus stop. When the bus dropped me off in the afternoon and when I walked to it in the morning there was creepy movements in the forest around the road.

Once in a while I would whip my head and body around fast enough to see a figure disappear behind a tree. I knew to a certain extent that something was in the woods, but I had been staying up late, actually catching up on my homework, so it must have been a deer or something, my tired eyes playing tricks on me. Or it could be those horror movies that I worshiped.

"Wynter," My teacher, Mr. Cull interrupted my thoughts, "You did the homework?" He was passing by everyone to check and see if theirs was done.

"Yeah and here's everything else that I haven't turned in since forever." I handed him my scrawled homework that I had spent hours on last night.

"Okay? You're in school, in class, taking notes," I had actually been kinda taking notes, "And you did all the homework you haven't been doing for weeks?" Mr. Cull shook his head in shock, accepting my homework to look over I guess, and walked away. Classmates around me looked on in mild surprise.

The other teachers I have had been saying the same thing, aside from the gym teacher, but she didn't count. Only study was left after this class, and I was going to skip. Chase had told me that I had to stay for all classes but seniors were allowed to skip last if they had study and a pass, which I did.

The history class passed at a pretty okay speed, my teacher just let us take notes by ourselves so I just laid my head on my desk listening to "I Just Laugh," by NeverShoutNever. The bell was a welcoming sound; I got up and left for my locker, throwing all the books from my arms to the top shelf. I wasn't going to do any homework tonight, nobody would be surprised.

By not bringing a purse or bag to school I had nothing to carry while I walked home, which I would be doing since the buses weren't here yet and I didn't have a car.

Once I had presented my pass, which I forged myself, to the office and walked out I remembered the seventy-degree heat. You may think that isn't so bad, but for me it was scalding. It was a fifteen-ish-minute ride because of the stops but only about three miles away from the school, to my house. Under normal weather conditions it was a rather pleasant walk, but in this temperature it would be pure torture.

I was only starting but ready to fall down and die. *I should have waited until the end of the day to take the bus*, I scolded myself.

Then there was a rip-roaring noise, louder than a car, softer than a truck, coming this way down the street. I didn't think anything of it until the noise slowed down and rode alongside me.

The driver's tinted helmet covered their face, but a hand bearing riding gloves lifted the visor, reveling those electric green eyes that I had run into a day before.

"Need a lift?" Zeek's deep voice asked through his helmet. In my mind I knew he was bad, but there was no internal conflict, I liked bad. Despite being in love with Chase I liked being around Zeek, even if this was only the second time.

"You have no idea how much I love you right now." I looked for how to get on, having never rid on one before. Zeek saw my confused face and laughed a deep throaty laugh.

He turned the bike off, put the kickstand down and threw his leg over it, standing only a foot in front of me. Taking his helmet off I was once again overcome by his looks. They were so different than what I was used to seeing; even Chase with his utter gorgeousness couldn't compete to Zeek in some aspects. Maybe that's just because he was my type, physically. Chase was still, well, Chase.

"Put this on." He didn't even wait for my permission before gently placing his helmet on my head. "Fit okay?" I nodded, feeling the out of place weight on my head bob back and forth.

"Not really, but it'll do. It's not like we're gonna crash." He followed up.

"How do I, um, get on?" I was embarrassed at my naive take on riding a motorcycle. Before I could ask again or even try myself I was in Zeek's arms.

"What are you doing?! Zeek!"

"Relax, I'm just putting you on. Jeez, overreaction you think?"

"Not really since I have no idea who you are and I have a skirt on!"

"Details, details."

"Don't look!" I screamed in his ear.

"No worries, I'm not looking. Besides you have shorts on." I sighed in relief.

"Wait, how do you know that?" A light blush coated Zeek's face, one that complemented his black hair well. He fondled his lip ring with his tongue, trying to think of an answer.

"While I was driving," he started slowly, "The wind may have picked up slightly." I blushed as well.

"Um, you can put me on the bike now." I giggled despite my embarrassment.

"Oh! Oh, yeah, right." Zeek put me on the back and turned the bike on.

"Where's your helmet?" I asked, now concerned about both of us falling off. I had a helmet, but he didn't.

"I don't need one."

"What if you fall off?"

"Don't worry, I'm a good driver, and besides I'm a little more durable than you, I'd be okay." After saying that he tore off, going down the road with a speed way over the limit. Shell shocked, I could barley move, and I was flailing about and shrieking with joy. Zeek took one of his hands and pulled mine from the air and moved it around his waste.

"Hold on!" He screamed over his shoulder, I barley heard him but pressed myself to his back as hard as I could. Next thing I knew he we were both screaming down the road as he navigated the dangerous turns.

I couldn't tell him to stop; I wouldn't even if I wanted to. It only took about a few minutes to get to my house, all the way up to the front door. He stopped in the shade, which I was very grateful for.

Zeek turned the motorcycle off and locked the handlebars. "You ready to get off?" I nodded in the negative, but still pulled the helmet off and gave it to him, how could anyone want to stop this?

Zeek laughed and got off himself, pulling me along side him. I went to take my first step but fell, unused to the shaky feeling when you first got off of the bike. Zeek grabbed my elbow and held me steady.

"Thanks."

"No problem, happens to everybody. It'll be easier next time."

"Next time?" He was assuming there would be a next time? I liked it. "Hey, you know what they say about assuming, Zeek."

"Yeah, if you assume it makes an ass out of you and me. But I kind of am an ass, so I think it works out quite nicely, don't you?" He laughed, and I caught a slight glimpse of white teeth.

"So, Zeek, how you holding up here in the heat? The sun?" My question caught him off-guard and his smile dropped fast, but he quickly recomposed himself.

"Fine, just fine, how about you, Wynter, you don't look so good." Spot on, I was pretty much melting.

"Not so good, you wanna come in for a drink or something?"

"That would be nice, thanks." He followed me in after I had unlocked the front door. I had left the air conditioning on and at a nice 65 degrees. Once inside both of us visibly relaxed, being out of the heat.

"Lemonade? Pink or normal? Or iced tea, soda, water, whatever."

"I'll have a Pepsi, if that's on hand." Good thing he isn't one of those shy houseguests, their kind bother me. So indecisive.

"Yup, right here." I went into the fridge and got us both one out, opening mine and drinking greedily.

"Diet?" Zeek cocked his pierced brow, I shrugged. "Please don't tell me you're one of those girls that are constantly dieting."

"Does it look like I care what others think?" I retorted.

"Maybe."

"Asshole, got the wrong kind, I normally don't have diet." I told him.

He pointed to the lip stud I had just given myself this morning. "You took my advice."

"Yeah, I suppose, it wasn't for them, though, it was for me."

"Good. I could see you getting another, you know, snake bites like these." He showed off his studs which were pretty hot, not that I would think that.

"I've been thinking about it, or a tongue one, now that would be freaking awesome." He stuck his own out, bearing a silver stud. Jealous. "Ah, okay, anything else I should see?"

"Anything else you wanna see?" I blushed, understanding the double meaning. Zeek was so unlike Chase in a lot of different ways, it was amusing to hear and see.

We sipped our sodas and talked for a while until Zeek looked at the clock on my stove and suddenly stood up, grabbing his helmet. "I have to go. Thanks for the drink." I stood up as well.

"What? Why, are you okay?" His tense expression immediately relaxed, though I could see it was only a front, a good one, but I was pretty good at reading into looks.

"Yeah, fine, I just didn't see the time, it's later than I thought." I didn't press him, that's all he was going to say.

"Yeah, okay then. See you around I guess?" This was only the second time seeing him but I believe we had grown close, considering my usual hatred towards anyone who wasn't Chase or Zelena. If I liked someone after the first day then they were a friend in my mind.

"Yeah," His voice grew soft, "Yeah, don't worry, Wynter, I'll be seeing you soon." He was hesitating, he looked like he wanted to say more but didn't know how to phrase it well.

"Oh spit it out."

"Just, Wynter just do me a favor and watch out for yourself, okay?" This time what he said caught me off-guard.

"Yeah, sure, fine, don't worry, I'm good. I have someone watching out for me." He muttered something that I couldn't hear, then he stepped towards me.

"Promise you'll watch yourself? You can't trust some people, you know?" I knew that already, his concern for me was startling, much like his eyes which were flashing at this very moment.

"Don't worry I can handle myself." I sounded harsh, I didn't mean to, but I don't like being underestimated. Zeek didn't comment back, only moved forward and planted a light kiss on my forehead.

"Until next time." His serious face paralyzed me, but then he swerved his head lower, capturing my lips with his own. I felt the tip of his tongue asking for entrance, and for a second I almost allowed him it, but then Chase's face flashed into my mind and I immediately pushed him away.

"Zeek!" I started pushing him out the front door. "What the hell?! What the hell was that for?" I was laughing though, we both were.

"Oh you liked it and you know it!"

"Go ride your bike, Zeek, walk away buddy before I go all kung-fu on your ass!" I gave him a final push and he was out the door. Walking towards his bike he unlocked it and turned the engine on.

"I'll be seeing you soon, Wynter!" He called, then he was gone, ripping down my driveway at killer speeds.

"Oh, God." I walked back in my house, locking the door behind me, you could never be too careful.

Putting the soda cans away, I thought of how weirdly attracted to Zeek I was. It was nothing like Chase, the mere thought of *him* rendered me senseless. I worshiped the guy, I had been for years. Not in a creepy stalker way, well I don't think so anyways. Zelena would argue that, but I was just so in love with him it was unfathomable.

Still the same, Zeek brought about a carefree way of life, it was fun, I'll admit. And still the same, my love for Chase didn't stop the tingling of my lips where he had kissed me, or the smile that graced my face as I cleaned up.

. . .

Shit, I still didn't ask him how he knew my name! And Chase didn't even come to see me today, again.

9

Bite Me

For you my body weeps,
For you my soul seeps.
Sucked from a cage of skin,
Nothing but one big sin.
-Nicole Evans

I woke up with a start to the sound of "Cassie" by Flyleaf the following morning, it was Saturday, finally! I hurried to get out of bed and into the shower, where I scrubbed myself until I was raw and smelling like my body wash. Passion fruit. I thought it was appropriate.

After the shower I ran into my room with a towel on to realize I didn't know what in God's name to wear. *How does one prepare for this? It probably isn't like fancy, since victims are just random mostly, but is it different if the person is willing? What if Chase ruins a shirt? Can't wear anything I like too much. Low collar for sure, I can't cover my neck. Socks and shoes won't matter.* I finally decided, so I pulled on mismatched socks and set my pink converse to the side. The multicolored shapes, including skulls and vampire bats, I had drawn onto them with Zelena now taunted me.

"I'm gonna kill someone." I spoke aloud. Nightmare blinked her gray eyes at me from my bed, stretched, then walked out of my room, "Thanks, Nightmare, now who's going to help me pick an outfit?" My question was left ignored.

I threw the towel to the ground and dressed myself with the basics. I went into the drawers of my disorganized bureau and pulled out a favorite pair of black skinny jeans. I decided against the usual studded belt, feeling as I may hurt him if it were possible, and opted for a smooth one with stars on it. Pulling on my shoes I searched the mess for a shirt I could wear.

"God, I should have planned this out beforehand." I never was a planner, probably never will be. I reached into the mess, my usual tactic, and pulled out five shirts, from those I would choose the one I would wear. Lucky for me most everything goes with black, which I almost always had on in some form.

The winner was a deep purple tank top, one of my favorite colors to wear. It looked like it would be on the cooler side, but I was never one to mind the cold anyway so all would be fine. I pulled a black camisole on then the purple tank over it.

"Now what?" I asked to myself. Since I hadn't seen Chase in such a while we didn't really even discuss Saturday. Today. I put my iPod on shuffle then fell into the music of "Midnattens Widunder" by Finntroll, not the calming effect I was looking for, but I was too far into the beat to care. Sliding on the linoleum floor in the kitchen I saw a note in Chase's hand.

    Wynter-

       Good morning, hope you slept well and all that jazz. It's Saturday, in case you forgot, though I doubt you have. I'll bet you were just destroying your room looking for clothes to wear. What you have on is perfect, and yes I'm saying that to keep the damage done to your home minimal, but also because it's a free-dress event. I'll be around the pond all day, so come whenever; we can do whatever you want. See you soon, that is unless you've chickened out.

-Chase

Chicken out? Please. *But how is this going to work? Do I just appear and get bitten or something? He did say that we could do whatever I wanted but I don't know . . .*

I grabbed my black and green zip-up jacket, put it on, and ran out the door, pausing only to lock it behind me.

Whenever he came inside, uninvited, he left it unlocked, the idiot. My iPod played a number of songs before I got to the part in the woods where I go in, I was walking slower than usual. I didn't stop to wonder why that was, but it didn't matter.

I saw the tree and a dark figure sitting about six feet high or so on some branches, Chase. Turning the music off I silently climbed to where he was sitting.

"Hey." I started cautiously.

"Didn't think you'd show this early."

"Really?" He didn't answer for a second until,

"Ok, yeah, I did." I giggled; I was so predictable to him. With anyone else it may have been troublesome, but it helped to have him know these things, saved time in some cases.

The two of us sat there for some time, neither having anything to say. The quiet was wonderful, just Chase and I. He was wearing a black jacket on top of his normal attire, though I don't know why, since he probably didn't feel cold at all. Everything was great until a weird gurgling sound came from my stomach.

"I swear to God that was my stomach." Blushing I bent over and hit it, trying to make the embarrassing noise stop and never happen again. Chase was looking at me weird.

"I know that was your stomach."

"Then what's with the hostile look?" It wasn't really hostile but he did look ticked off to a certain degree.

"The look is for the fact that you didn't eat breakfast, Wynter, because you were rushing out here too fast and forgot, *again*." I had forgotten how much that bothered him, but it was an honest mistake, I had just wanted to see Chase.

"Eh, I'll eat later, let's just hang out or do something." He sighed at my lack of caring about eating breakfast. But an idea brightened in his eyes and his frown turned into a smile.

"Yeah, okay, we'll go do something," I was about to sigh in relief at the change of topic until he finished his sentence, "We'll go out to breakfast."

"Awh man, really?" But I already knew the answer.

"You complain that I don't go out in public with you but as soon as I do you don't want to go, what's with that?"

"I just don't wanna eat breakfast food!" I never eat breakfast for a reason.

"You'd rather have cookies or something, am I right?"

"Maybe." Then his smirk, the one that I loved and hated, appeared, along with a devilish look on his face. Soon as I figured out what he was going to do, Chase pulled me off of the branch we had been sitting on and launched us out of the tree.

"Oh, c'mon!" It wasn't the first time he had done this, but I never could figure out why he always landed, with me especially, so well on the ground. Knowing now that he was just showing off his vampire skills both made me laugh and want to hit him.

"Show-off." I muttered when he let go of my arms.

"Oh you liked it and you know it." His words brought me back to just yesterday, when Zeek called it out to me after leaving with his stolen kiss. A mix between a blush at the memory and a scowl at the fact that I was remembering this now when I was with Chase crossed my face.

"Okay, okay maybe it was a little fun," His coal eyes seemed to twinkle, "Now let's go!" I urged him out of the woods and soon we were walking on the deserted road.

Neither of us had a car, I couldn't afford one and he thought it useless when he never really went anywhere. Walking or taking a bus was the only way we got anywhere.

"Where you thinking of going?" I asked.

"Isn't there that little coffee shop not too far from your school?" He didn't wait for an answer, "I thought maybe there, that alright?" I nodded yes, it wasn't a far walk, to my dismay, and it was sort of cloudy out. The place Chase was talking about was nice; Zelena and I had often gone to during studies or whenever we wanted a snack. How he knew of it, I'm not sure; I didn't want to ask though.

Our walk was mostly spent in comfortable silence, with some small talk here and there. It wasn't until we were passing Nightingale Park, a block away from the shop, that a ripping noise flooded the street beside us. We both turned to see the source of the noise, a motorcycle going way too fast drove past us, the driver turned their head for only a split second, but I knew it was Zeek.

"Jesus, think he could slow down? Young people these days." I heard an older guy mutter who was walking in front of us. Chase rolled his eyes and whispered, "The reason he's so pissed off is because he used to have one and can't ride anymore." I didn't know if that was a guess or his super vampire skills told him, but I laughed and nodded in agreement just the same.

We walked in and got a table right away, I think the waitress put us ahead of other people waiting because of Chase. The coffee shop was surprisingly full, even for a Saturday morning, though by now I suppose it was roughly twelve by now.

"Hello my name is Anna; can I start you off with anything?" An older, too-skinny waitress with overdone makeup flashed her cigarette stained teeth at us. I'm fine with people smoking, hell I do once in a while myself, but when you smoke and don't brush your teeth and drink *way* too much coffee, it becomes a problem.

"Wynter?"

"Um, yes, I'll have a raspberry tea, if you don't mind." I closed the menu and set it on the table.

"And you, sir?" Anna looked away from me, turning to Chase.

"Earl Gray for me, and do you have any chocolate pastries?" That was odd; Chase normally ate lemon or vanilla. She laughed; it was a raspy, unnatural sound, like one of a dying cat. I saw Chase shudder.

"Yes, chocolate chip muffin sound alright? Should I bring something healthier too? At your age should be eating eggs! Healthy, healthy eggs."

"Yes, she'll have one of those," He said, pointing to me, "And I'll have a slice of lemon pound cake." I so called that.

"Is that all? No eggs?"

"Yes, that's all, thank you." He turned away and shot me a look. *Help me!* He mouthed.

"Are you sure, I think you need some eggs. I love them. You know I used to have a chicken farm when I was younger!" She trailed off, clearly caught up in the good old days.

"Yes, yes he is sure!" I stood up, pushing my chair back behind me, "Now will you please stop talking about eggs to my boyfriend it's *really* weirding me out! Go take our orders to the kitchen, there you go!" Most of the people in the shop had heard me, though they just turned back to their meals, ignoring me. Except one older lady in red who, after watching the waitress leave in a huff, turned to me,

"She talked about eggs to me too, I wish I had thought of that." She said with a wink, and then turned back to her coffee. I sat back down, pulling my chair closer to the table and looked at Chase.

"Quite the display there, Wynter." I blushed; I went a little overboard I guess. But it was weird, who talks about eggs that much? "Good thing you're not the jealous type, right?" I had told him that I wasn't quite a while ago, I was surprised he remembered.

"Shut up." I mumbled in my defense. "That wasn't jealousy that was me saving you from a huge creeper."

"What was that part about your boyfriend . . . ?" He taunted.

"Very funny Chase, I had to get her to leave *somehow* didn't I?"

"Well you did quite nicely then, I think anyways." His mouth formed a little half smile and he winked.

"Oh laugh it up now, next time I'm leaving you with her." I wasn't serious, of course, I couldn't stand to watch that go down, and she would probably have him buy a chicken or something. However I think I put on a nice façade.

"I don't think she'll be back any time soon."

"You'd be surprised with the ignorance of people like her." I corrected him.

"And you know nothing about ignorance, right? You always think things through before you dive in head first." *Me? Yeah, right. I go with my gut feeling towards things and proud of it!*

"Oh, you know I think things though. I would never do something like promise a blood sacrifice, or say, allowing a guy to jump out of a tree with you or silly things like that." I had meant the examples to be light hearted but Chase's face was just a little too serious.

"Did you think at all before you told me I could bite you?" His voice was low but I could hear him just fine. Hurt, I think, flashed in his eyes.

"Oh, no, no, no Chase. I was just saying that to say it, it was a joke, don't worry." He didn't lighten up.

"You don't have to do that, you know, if you don't want me to bite you, just say the word, it won't hurt my feelings." But I could see it would have.

"I honestly don't mind, at all, promise."

"Don't mind doing it borders not wanting to, am I right?" Of course he way, he always was.

"I want you to." I said it just strong enough to bite my tongue to keep from blushing, though I'm pretty sure I did anyway. He face did a 180 and soon he was smirking at me again.

"Don't say a word." I warned him, and he didn't, we just sat there until our food came. Anna dropped it off, in a daze, and hurried on her way. *Maybe she's on something* . . . I smirked at her back, though I didn't do it so well considering Chase was shaking his head and chuckling at my immature behavior.

"What's so funny?" I asked, sipping the tea. It was too hot and I scalded my tongue. I quickly scarfed down a piece of muffin to try and cool it off, didn't work.

"You." I accepted this answer and took another bite of muffin, followed by another. Guess I really was hungry.

"You should have another," Chase commented when he saw it was almost gone already, "Today will be tolling on you, since it's your first time being bitten." I lowered my eyes to the table, it was hard to talk to him and not blush.

"I've told you before, don't hide your face from me." He lifted my head and made me look at him. I distracted myself by asking another question.

"What happens after?" He knew what I was talking about and saved me humiliation by pretending not to.

"You," he began, "Will most likely faint." Oh. I didn't know that part.

"'Cause it's the first time it's happened?"

"Yeah probably, I don't know for sure, just happens I suppose. All the people I bite faint, though that may be the me willing it part, not sure."

"What about the second time, or after that?"

"Are you volunteering for more than today?" He countered my questions with one of his own, oh, was he good or what?

"Maybe." We continued on like that until the food was gone. Chase paid at the kitchen bar and we left, not wanting to run into Anna again.

"So do you bite more girls or guys?"

"Girls, mostly only girls. Why, jealous again?" He looked worried about me being so though.

"No. Sorta. Yeah. Why?"

"I've told you that it's a sexual feeling right?"

"Yeah."

"Well I'm not knocking gay people but I'm straight and that's really weird to me. Though I would if necessary."

"That makes a surprisingly lot of sense."

"It should Wynter, I happen to be able to think things through logically."

"I hate you." He wrapped his arm around my shoulders and reassured me that I didn't.

~ ~ ~ ~ ~

Walking home was less eventful after that, but my insides churned. It had to be soon, what else was there to do that wasn't just to prolong the point of today? We took our time and eventually made our way to the pond and our tree. I don't know how long we were there; I was lying on the ground while Chase had his back against the tree, but I do know we were waiting for the rain that was promised to come and or the inevitable. Finally, as the first drops of rain fell, I swallowed my nervousness and sat up, moving to sit next to Chase.

"I, um, don't know how to go about this . . ." I admitted, playing with my fingers, he grabbed them and held them still.

"Then simply do what you want." I let go of everything and did just that. Without being pulled or prompted to, as it normally was, I got up and sat on Chase's lap. At first I just rested my head against his strong chest, but I knew it would only last so long. He probably wouldn't tell me just how much, or if it put him in pain, but he thirsted.

"I love you."

It wasn't planned, the words just freed themselves from the cage I had kept in my heart and soared out of my mouth, then hung in the air.

Next thing I knew Chase's mouth was on mine, the first kiss he gave me led to another and another. The kisses started off light and inviting but as the rain fell harder around us the kisses became rougher and more demanding. The tree we sat under kept us drier than around it, but soon I stopped noticing. It was getting harder to keep my eyes open, which I had been.

I didn't want to close my eyes, Chase already had, but I never wanted to lose sight of him, fearing that he would slip away. I felt the sharp tips of his fangs with my tongue as he probably felt the dull tips of mine with his own. My arms were around his back, my hands in his hair, as his were entangled in my curls. Lungs burning, I tried to catch my breath when I could, not wanting to stop kissing him, even for the air that I needed.

The rain was pouring when Chase pulled me back, letting us both catch our breath. I didn't take my eyes off his face, and he didn't take his eyes off of mine either. Slowly then he kissed my ear, I shivered, his kisses descended then to my mouth, my jaw line, then down my neck, to my throat.

"You're sure?" He looked up briefly. I nodded, having lost my voice to the power of lust. Then I felt the tips of his four fangs touch my neck. I grabbed hold of his shirt, inside his open jacket, and held tight, preparing myself. I was as nervous as if I were losing my virginity to him or something. It seemed that important, to give away to the boy that I love. Nor sure why exactly, but it's the truth.

He nibbled on the skin before biting down hard. There was a prick, like that of a needle, and then he was sucking my blood.

It was better than I had imagined it would be, nothing Chase would have said could have prepared me for it. I closed my eyes and lost myself to the pleasure of having the one I love drink his fill of me. Colors of every hue, every shade, passed before my eyes. It was only seconds, but it felt like hours, not in the bad way that is often implied with this statement, but in the way that meant eternity was nothing if it was spent like this with Chase.

I could tell he was enjoying himself too; the slow drinking that he started out with at first gave way to greedy sucking at my neck. I felt a hickey forming, but didn't care; I loved it, in fact. A hickey would just be proof of what was happening, and a mark on my body that would tell everyone that I was his.

Then, too soon, I felt dizzy and knew he would stop in little time, much to my disappointment. Not long after the feeling came over me the pleasurable drinking slowed down until it stopped all together. Chase's fangs pulled out and I saw him wipe his mouth on the back of his hand, having opened my eyes a bit. My grip had since loosened on his shirt and I faintly noticed his other hand supporting my back.

"You full?" I managed to get out, feeling the darkness coming, as he said it would. He answered my question with a chaste kiss. I felt him stand up; holding me in his arms, and let myself fall into the darkness. For a minute after closing my eyes I felt the rain on me as he carried me home and heard his voice, ever so faintly.

"Thank you, Wynter."

. . .

You're welcome.

10

A Pool of Repentance

Corrupted hearts ban together,
Float with me and I won't tell
No longer light, as a feather
Let me weigh you down to hell.
-Nicole Evans

Sunlight flicked onto my face the morning after, soft and caressing. It was Sunday, early in the morning, I probably should have slept more, but every few minutes a throb in my neck would reawaken me. Chase was on the couch, actually asleep, which was surprising. Vampires almost never needed sleep; he had told me before, turns out that when they did, though, they were *gone*.

I slipped out of bed around five and decided to take a walk around in the woods to catch the early morning. I was so happy even the sun was alright.

Random songs were playing from the iPod in my pocket, but I couldn't concentrate long enough to tell which ones. Then one switched to "If I Was Your Vampire," by Marilyn Manson, and I started laughing.

The dark song with meaningful lyrics got me thinking about heaven and hell. I wasn't a very religious person, seeing as though I never went to church and prayed rarely, but I had to wonder what was going to happen to Chase. He would live for two centuries give or take some, all the while taking blood from humans; he also mentioned that he had killed someone before. Add being an 'undead' vampire who cheated the system of life on top of that, and Chase wasn't looking so hot. Or at least his soul wasn't.

He probably doesn't care, not one to be thinking of that sort of thing. But a thought nagged at my mind: *What if I don't see Chase after we both die?* The question struck me like splinters of ice, then colder more foreboding thoughts followed. *What if I die, go to heaven, hell or wherever, and have to spend eternity as a soul without Chase? Unable to live without him, but unable to die, being already dead.* By the time I realized that I was slowly descending into one of my moods where I question the meaning of life relentlessly, it was already too late.

I stood where I was, staring into nothingness, seeing blackness around me, trying to think of what would happen. The thought of having an eternity somewhere without Chase was too hard to think about, yet I continued to do so.

A loud honk sounded and I looked up, startled, I had chosen to stand in the middle of a suburban road, lucky for me close to no cars traveled along it so only one car was being held up. The honk yanked me back to reality in time to get out of the way onto the side of the road, and wipe the tears that had lightly cascaded down my face in the process of my thinking.

"He'll be fine." But I had to confirm it out loud to even partially convince myself. *What could I do to help him? It's not like I could get him to go to church with me or something . . .* But that thought struck me; church! Maybe he wouldn't go, but I still could! It was perfect, it was a Sunday morning and I had nothing to do anyways, why not go to church and pray for Chase's soul? *'Cause you've never been before, maybe that's why.* A voice sounded in my head, and it was right. I pushed the thought aside, churches don't barricade people out, do they? Well yeah, they probably do, but not in a small town like this. Regardless I switched directions and went to change into 'church clothes.'

~~~~~

Chase still wasn't up when I snuck back into the house, man oh man he was asleep! Usually he heard everything, every little noise I made, now, not so much. I could probably stomp up the stairs and he wouldn't notice, which I proceeded to try, of course. This resulted in me stepping on one of the obnoxiously long neon pink laces coming from the black combat boots I had put on. I tripped forward and heard a crack, the sound my cheekbone made whilst smacking against the edge of the stairs, from there I slid down to the ground floor.

"*Shit!*" I whisper yelled, rolling on the floor, withering in pain. A flare shot up from the bottom of my face to the top of it, I grinded my teeth in fury at my stupidity.

After the flaming pain dulled down to a pulsing throb to join the every continuing throbbing on my neck, I army crawled from my place on the floor to peek around the corner. Chase, still on the couch, barely twitched his head, I sighed. "You're an idiot Wynter, you know that?" *Yes, I know that.*

Feeling warm blood ooze from my cut cheek I grabbed a bag of ice from the fridge and headed up, *carefully*, to my room. This would be just lovely for my first time going to church. Terrific.

~ ~ ~ ~ ~

I was late getting to the white building; it took a while to find something appropriate for a holy place and cover-up the not-as-bad-as-it-looked cut. Not to mention the hickey, the purple hickey with puncture wounds in it. I settled on a long black skirt and a white high-collared blouse I didn't know I had. *Aunt Emily must have left it, we're about the same size, I guess.* At least the skirt fit, the blouse was a little tight for such a place, but I wasn't planning on socializing with anyone anyway, so it wouldn't be a problem.

Quietly letting myself in the front doors I went up to the balcony as to not disturb the minister who was already talking. It was a striking place, really, old beauty, which I personally found the best in many cases, churches especially.

Women, men and children all sat in the white pews with red cushions down below me. Gold thread adorned the edges of the seats, giving the fabric a shimmering appearance. Some of the people were dressed up more fancy, other just nicely. There were intricately designed stain glass windows depicting the life of Jesus in five scenes. His birth, baptism, sacrifice, death, and finally, his resurrection.

The balding man clad in black with crosses surrounding him asked everyone to stand; the congregation complied as one being. Hymns were sung, one after another, followed by a beautiful classical piece by their organist. An older woman walked up to the front of the church and after reciting something called the Call to Worship she led the Lord's Prayer.

Soon after the minister took her place, asking us to bow our heads in silence, to pray for loved ones and to keep some aforementioned people in our thoughts. I bowed my head, hands clasped in an effort to make this as official as possible.

Dear God, I began, *I know I don't come here . . . ever . . . but I really need your help. I've been thinking about Chase and how he has cheated you and your power in many ways. I apologize for that but there is nothing I can do but believe in you and your help. Please bless Chase's soul. He isn't evil, only a good person, it isn't his fault for what he is. Being a vampire wasn't his choice,* I prayed, though I don't really know this for a fact, *he's kind; a gentleman. When I die, please, if I go to heaven or hell, send Chase there also, when his time is up . . . if not that then let me go to where he will.*

I could have said more, I would have said more, but the minister gave us a limited time to pray on our own. Maybe this wasn't the place for me, there was still so much more. I could just come here when everyone was gone. Or find another place to pray. *Who are you kidding; you'll forget to pray.* I told myself.

Seeing as though the praying in silence was the only reason I was here, and it had already finished, I took my leave. Using my sneaking-out-of-the-house moves that I acquired before I was on my own I got out. I was close to sure that nobody had noticed me leave anymore than they noticed me enter.

That could have gone better. I thought to myself, stretching and shielding my eyes from the sun that was trying its hardest to break through the clouds. *But I suppose it could have gone worse, too.* Now that I was out of the building I took my long curls out of the high ponytail I had put it into, shook my head, and let the black fall into place.

"I should dye it again." I started talking to myself. I had added some pink streaks not too long ago; it would be cool to try again. "No, what I need is more clothes, with high collars. Or a necklace, this thing would be obnoxious to walk around with all day . . ." I poked my neck, it sort of hurt.

The sun was coming out on the way home. Not way too bright or warm, just right. Well, for the sun anyways. I took out my cell—no new messages. *I wonder if Chase is up. Or would he call if he were?*

There wasn't anything to do now, Chase is asleep or something and Zelena was probably at home watching her little brother.

I could go swimming. Yeah, that isn't such a bad idea. Sometimes when I'm alone or bored I'll go swimming at the pond. It's quite refreshing really. Chase doesn't know I do, I don't think. Nobody does. I love Chase and Zelena, however swimming alone in silence is just perfection. So I went home and got my bathing suit.

~~~~~

Chase had been gone when I got back. Figures, he probably saw that I wasn't there and decided to take off. We aren't the kind of people who needed to be updated on each other's whereabouts 24/7. I grabbed my rainbow cheetah print bathing suit from the back of my closet and put it on under a hoodie, then grabbed a towel, and started out.

"I wonder if it'll be weird between us." I spoke. "It shouldn't be though, he's my best friend. Or what? Hmm, what *are* we?" Seriously. I've said I love you-"

I did.

I told him I loved him, did I not? How did that slip my mind? So many important things did. And, and he said it back. Didn't he? No wait, he didn't. *That's disappointing. But he did kiss me a lot after that; then there was the bite . . . I guess that means the same thing to him.*

I stripped down to my suit and put my clothes in a pile not long after I left. The water would be cool, but its never bothered me before. I don't do that go in slowly thing; it just made the shock more prolonged. Instead I dove in, a shallow dive so I wouldn't break my neck.

"Damn that is frickin *cold!*" I yelped. The iciness of the pond was surprising. Colder than I thought it would be. "Man maybe this wasn't such a good idea." *I need to see someone about this whole talking to myself thing.* As I soaked for a little longer though, it wasn't as bad.

Dead man's float was the way to go when you're alone. It was so peaceful. I looked up and saw the sky through the trees; leaves fell once in a while. Then I closed my eyes and could imagine anything I wanted was above me. I always wanted to come when it was night, but it would be too dangerous. Even I knew that.

I fell asleep in the water. Well, not fast asleep, but I was resting my eyes for a long time. You know, that place where you're awake but can't tell how fast the time goes by, and you can go anywhere in your mind.

I was with my parents, before they left. It was one of the very few memories I have of them when they were happy. There was never any fighting, just constant sighing, which may have been worse. I never knew why they sighed; if there were fights at least I would know how come. But the past is the past, and I moved on.

I was with Zelena, the first day we met. Middle School Detention, 6th grade to be exact. It was one of my first; it was for sure her first. I don't remember exactly what I did, but they handed them out for one missing homework, so probably that. Nothing else really happened, we were both loners and just sort of stuck together since. Safety in numbers and all, not that two was a high number, but we worked with what we had.

Chase, Chase, Chase. Memories flew by of big and little moments together, and I smiled.

A rustle in the trees brought me back to real time, normal time. I sat up, touching my feet to the gravel and leaves on the bottom of the pond. But nothing was there. *My imagination. Or maybe I was deeper into whatever that is than I thought.*

But there it was again. Just a faint noise, someone or something stepping on a leaf, a stick; whatever it was, was too big to be a squirrel.

"Chase?" No answer. "Hey come out, Jackass!" Another crunch, followed by silence.

"C'mon, seriously! You're gonna make me look like one of those stupid chicks from all the movies! Calling out to a supposed nothing. Here, I'll make it better." I put my hands to my face in mock terror.

"Oh, um, hello? Is-is anybody out there? Hello? Who's there? Come out!" I looked around like one of those dip-shits from the horror scenes. "But really, Chase, either go away or come out." Still nothing.

"Fine, be that way." I went back to floating, there wasn't anything to be afraid of.

I got out of the water probably ten minutes after that, and went to dry off. It was frigid out in the air, even worse than the water itself. Walking towards where I placed my things, I saw my clothes, but no towel.

"*Chase*! Get out here with my towel *now* it is *freezing* out!" I shouted into the trees. I guess he did know that I swam here; he always found things out without me telling him.

Heavy footsteps in the woods came my way. *God his jokes are just too funny. Not.* I crossed my arms to keep the shivers at bay, plus I was embarrassed to be in a swimsuit. Before I could see Chase come out I grabbed my hoodie to hold in front of me.

"Well I thought it was sort of funny." Said the voice from behind a tree, but it wasn't Chase's voice. Zeek stepped out from the woods.

"Huh? What are *you* doing here Zeek?"

"I dunno, why are you here?"

"What do you mean 'I dunno'? This is my place!"

"I don't see your name on it." He retorted, toying with my towel.

"Nice, Zeek, don't you think that's a little juvenile? And give me my towel back I'm freezing my tatas off!"

"Really? I didn't think that was possible, can I see?" He laughed and threw me the thing.

"Funny boy." I dropped the hoodie and caught the towel, then turned around to pat myself dry. I heard him take a sharp intake of breath. Turning back, Zeek was staring at me, looking horrified.

"What? Zeek, what? What's the matter?" He was staring at my neck. *Damn, I didn't even think of that. Must look awkward to him.* "Openly staring much? Really."

"Who did that to you?" His voice was as cold as the water I had just stepped out of.

"None of your business, man, stop looking!" I finished drying and put my hoodie on. He walked fast towards where I was standing and planted his feet firmly in front of me.

"I asked, *who did that to you?*" There was glint in his eyes. All of a sudden he looked dangerous, like he wanted to kill someone.

"My," I hesitated, "My boyfriend, okay!? God that is *so* not any of your business!" He quickly grabbed my hair and pushed the hood of my sweatshirt down, revealing the bite mark nestled in the purple bruise. I pushed him away, backing up a little.

"What the hell, Zeek!? What is the matter with you?" I pulled my wet spirals over my shoulders and readjusted my hoodie. "What is your problem? You've never acted like this before." *Maybe I don't know him as well as I thought I did.*

"He's started. Already, he's started." Mumbled words, I couldn't really pick them up.

"What?"

"Chase . . . Lucius . . . you bastard, I won't let you get another one." With that said, Zeek ran off into the woods, in the direction away from the road.

What the hell!?

Where was Chase? We seriously needed to talk. I bolted in the direction of my house.

~ ~ ~ ~ ~

When I got home, Chase wasn't there. He didn't come over for the rest of the day, nor the night. I went to bed with so many unanswered questions. And the one at the top of my mind was this:

How does Zeek know Chase, who's Lucius, and what did he mean by "get another one"?

11

A Damned Family

Scream. The recessive pain rears its head.
After the disaster, it will keep coming back.
Love destroyed, vanquished, gone.
My heart shatters, my heart shatters.
-Nicole Evans

Chase was avoiding me. It was Monday already. I didn't see him on Saturday, after the afternoon with Zeek, or all of Sunday. I've gone without seeing him for a few days before, but he has always told me.

What the hell? He can't just suck me blood then leave. Should have at least found a phone somewhere *and called me. Didn't he say that it was a sexual experience? I though it was. That makes him look like a player. A guy who sleeps with a girl then gets up and leaves without a word. Expect with drinking blood . . . weird scenario.*

Sluggishly, I walked to the bus stop. Even my music wasn't helping my mood. "Frantic," by Metallica tried to cheer me up, but nothing worked.

Is that all he wanted? Is he gone for good? That couldn't be it. At least not only it, he's my best friend, he isn't going anywhere.

I got to the bus stop and pulled myself aboard with a pace that made the driver want to drag me on and yell at me. I sped up just enough for him to close the doors and start moving.

Nobody was on the bus. By nobody, I mean Zeek. Not that I should have expected his cycle to break down again. I was mad at him, but maybe he could have told me something. Like where the hell Chase is or what the hell he meant on Saturday.

Who did he mean by Lucius? I had never heard that name before in my life. It didn't sound like a name anyone would give to their kid in this time and age. Then again Wynter wasn't a normal name either.

I sighed and watched the trees snap by as green flashes. I tried counting them to pass the time and get my mind off of everything. It sort of worked because the school came into view.

Where is he? Where is my Chase? And why do I have such a bad feeling?

~ ~ ~ ~ ~

There are these twins in my school, fraternal for sure. They're friends with a few girls from some of my classes. Sometimes I wonder where they went, 'cause I don't seem them anymore. One used to be in my German class, I cheated off of her sometimes. The other was in a study I have; she did her homework, unlike me. They were opposites in attitude, really. Wherever they went, I probably won't find out, I'm too lazy to look into it.

Sometimes I see two girls in my gym class. One blondie, one brownie; one curly hair, one straight. The blonde one dances; I know this because I often hear a comment about it. The brownie plays volleyball, I believe, only because she's really good at it. They don't seem to have very high self-esteem, but I think that they should. Those two are gorgeous, and nice on top of it.

There is this girl, this *loud* girl. She dances a lot; her iPod is always in her ear. I'm not sure what's with her, honestly. Every time I see her she's with this black-hair chick. Her knockers are really *huge* and they're always kissing.

There are unicorn drawings all over a math classmates notebooks. I don't know her that well but I've heard stories about what goes on outside of school, but she keeps smiling; it makes me happy that people can always seem to find a reason to smile.

There is this curly blonde. She dresses like I do, all black all the time. Well not *all* black, but you know the style I'm talking about. She always finds ways to listen to her iPod during class. She seems like the odd man out, most the other girls are preppy-ish.

But all the same those girls are friends.

Why are they the ones I observe when I'm bored? When I'm depressed about something? Because a lot of people don't like 'em, they don't think all of them should be friends, but the girls don't conform to make people accept them. Well, most of them don't anyway. That brings my mood up on most days, I don't know why though. Observing people who shouldn't go together, but do, is really amusing.

I spent the day observing them in the halls, in the classes we have together, and during lunch. There's something that's just sort of *off* about each of them, if you look hard enough. Divorce, cheating, overbearing, lying, deceiving, abused, pressured, depressed, or something of that nature. I can relate to each of them in some way.

The curly blondes have tried talking to me before; they were either trying to make a new friend or trying to be nice. I didn't brush them off 'cause one is like me in quite a few ways and the other is just too cute to upset. They hold hands *everywhere* they go, no matter where they go.

The emo one, the one like me, calls the taller one her Little Ballerina, or her Fishy. I've heard some funny things about her, like the time she punched a guy in the face for making fun of and pinching her Little Ballerina.

I thought about talking to them, but I don't think I could have joined their group of friends. Big groups make me uncomfortable. But maybe I'll join just those two once in a while, if Zelena doesn't show up for some reason, like today. She's sick.

~ ~ ~ ~ ~

A sinking feeling has been following me around all day. Like the sort of feeling you'd get if you saw a shadow behind you as you entered a dark alleyway. Like something was coming; something really, *really* bad. I don't know what it is. Even observing that interesting group of people didn't help me. I though I was just sad, but it's something else.

Chase was in trouble.

That's all I can think of, because he hadn't come to visit me, and I haven't seen him since Saturday morning.

The bus ride home has been shit so far because I want to know I would see him as soon as I walked in my house, but at the same time I know I won't. But then since I "knew" I wouldn't see him, maybe I would. It's a vicious cycle that I couldn't really explain.

But what can I say to him when I do see him? "Oh hey, thanks for totally ditching me." I want to hit him, but I know I can't. Well not so much can't as won't.

The ancient and very dangerous bus finally stopped and I raced off of it. With a groan and a puff of smog, it pulled away and I was faced with my driveway.

"Nothing to do but pray he's there I guess." More talking to myself. Should I get that looked into? Yes. Regardless, I started walking.

~ ~ ~ ~ ~

Upon getting the house, the first thing I heard was the shrill ring of my phone. I always leave it at home, just 'cause I'm forgetful. I grabbed at it, and saw that I didn't have the number.

"Hello?"

"Wynter? It's Chase."

"*Where the hell are you?!*" I screamed into the phone, he's such a damn idiot.

"I called you like six times, Wynter, it's not my fault you forgot your phone at home again."

"Whatever, I'm stupid, we've got that. Now where are you?"

"Not too far away," Came his calm voice. "I'm going to come over so we can talk, is that alright?" *Oh shit.*

"That doesn't sound good." My anger drained from me and was replaced with the panicked beating of my heart.

What's this about? It sounds like it's going to be really bad . . .

"It's okay, I just wanted to warn you that I'm a little, um, bruised, and I knew if I just came over that you'd freak out before I could tell you that I'm okay."

"You're *what*? Bruised? Are you okay? Did you get into a fight? Did you win? Do you need to go to the hospital or-"

"Wynter, shut up, really, this is why I called to warn you instead of just coming over. Be there in a little."

"When?" No response.

"Hello? Chase when are you gonna be here?" Still no response.

"You did *not* hang up on me!" I checked the phone, he defiantly did. "Damn you!"

I slammed the phone on a table and angrily paced for a little. I was muttering to myself about how stupid he was but finally got bored.

May as well grab something to eat and watch something, maybe a show other than shit reality TV is on. God knows all that's on those programs are drunken sluts making fools of themselves.

Kicking off my boots I grabbed a pomegranate, my obsession, and plopped down on the sofa; cutting into the red and juicy fruit.

I ate and waited around for twenty of so minutes, preparing for the worst. He's never gotten into a fight before. If he has, he hasn't told me and he certainly hasn't gotten bruises or anything from it.

"Chase, you bastard, I won't let you get another one." Didn't Zeek just say that a few days ago? Damn, I'll bet it was him! He's the bastard, I sware if he hurt Chase I'm going to kill *him!*

"Wynter, open up!" Banging followed Chase's voice and I jumped over the couch, making a mad dash to the door.

"It's open!" I called as I grabbed the doorknob and let him in. I looked up at him and didn't see anything at all on his face. He gave me a half smile, showing off his top fang a bit and turned, showing me the other side of his face. He gammed his thumb, pointing to a bloody bruise that took up a good portion of the other side of his face.

"How you like it, Wynter? I kicked *ass* to get this!" Smug boy, so typical.

"God, Chase, you're gonna get yourself killed!" Have to admit, it looks pretty badass though.

"Naw, I won't. You like it or what?"

"Really manly, which is what you were going for I assume?"

"You should see the other guy!" He laughed, God I loved that sound.

"Speaking of which who *is* the other guy?"

"Well first off," he started walking into the kitchen, "Hi. Secondly, do you have a drink?" He was shifting through the cupboards.

"Hey and no probably not. I don't drink much." Which was a lie he would probably call me out on.

"Yeah, okay Wynter. Now where is it? Anything really." He continued looking through all the places in my kitchen for something.

"It's gone actually, why you want a drink it's like four o'clock or something, I don't know."

"This thing on my face looks damn cool but it hurts like a sonofabitch."

"Oh get out Chase!" I pushed him away from the kitchen and lead him to the bathroom, "You don't drink 'cause something hurts, you drink for other reasons; you take a pain reliever when something hurts." I opened the mirror drawer and got him three pills.

"Oh yum, they're even coated with cherry flavor Wynter, thanks." But he took them from my hand anyway.

"Hey!" I raised my voice, "they taste good shut up Chase! Sarcastic idiot."

"You know you aren't suppose to eat them like candy, don't you?" Popping them and swallowing without water, Chase shoved a few more in his pocket. For later, I think. Then he started out to the couch where the TV was still on.

"I know, it's just better for when I need them, I'll eat normal candy when I want to."

"How do you not have a thousand cavities yet?"

"I dunno."

He turned to the TV and watched whatever was on, while I watched his face, trying to imagine him in a fight. I could and it was hot. Fights sort of turn me on, I'm not going to lie, and I would have loved to see it go down. Though I'd be freaking out like crazy at the same time I know.

"So who was the other guy?" Better not be Zeek. Chase shifted and looked at me for a second.

"Yeah, about that. There's a long-ass story I've gotta tell you, I suppose."

~~~~~

"Alright, Once Upon a Time-"

"Chase, really?"

"Fine. So here I am, a vampire. I was born a vampire by my parents, who were both vampires as well."

"Really? Well where are they now?"

"Dead. They had me late in life and . . . died . . . when I was much younger. But no matter, vampires don't need their parents for very long. After a few years of age, we can fend for ourselves. Most leave when they turn eight-ish because by then they know everything they need to."

"Like animals?"

"Weird, but yeah. We're not humans, we don't need to rely on parents for so long."

"I don't."

"Most of your kind do though." *My* kind. For some reason I didn't like being classified like that.

"Anyway, before they died my mom cheated on my dad, which was bad enough on it's own. But to make matters worse he found out because my idiot mom got pregnant. Then she decided to *keep* the baby for God knows why, and gave me a half brother."

"You have a brother?! Who is he, where does he live, do you get along-"

"Wynter, I'm getting there. Problem is that the dude my mom banged was human. Producing a half vampire half human kid thing. My dad obviously noticed that it wasn't his, found out whom my mom was with, and killed him. Then he went sort of crazy, both of them did actually. They tried to get along for a while, while raising this human-vampire mix but things just kept getting worse. I was two when my brother was born, and from then until I was seven I had to watch him 'cause my parents to grow crazier and crazier."

"What do you mean by crazy?"

"First it was just fighting a lot, not really crazy. But then they would leave for days and come back in the same unwashed clothes, caked with blood. They started killing humans not for sustenance, but so they wouldn't kill each other. Apparently my mom really loved that guy my dad killed. She never looked at my brother, she told me once that they looked just like each other."

"Poor kid . . ."

"No, everything is his fault. Everything is. When I was seven my parents . . . well they finally snapped. My brother was an innocent five year old, nobody had cared to tell him who his dad was, and he overheard one of the daily fights. He heard that my dad wasn't his dad and asked who was, and that just killed them. Literally. The fight started turning physical like it did a lot, but this time neither one of them let up. They both bled out in the end." I couldn't think of what to say to that. His parents killed each other when he was seven because of a . . . well an affair.

"Oh . . . violent." Brilliant.

"Well you humans do stuff like that too, crime of passion, remember?"

"Oh yeah I guess you're right." We sat in silence until I interrupted it,

"Do you miss them?"

"So here I am," He ignored my last question, "Stuck with a kid brother who isn't enough of a human to ditch at an orphanage but not vampire enough to raise as one. I didn't know what to do with him. I did the best I could, but he couldn't keep up with me, and I could never forgive him, I mean he killed my parents!" Chase started shaking, looking real worked up, and it was frightening.

"Everything I did seemed to make matters worse. Then when I was fifteen and he was thirteen he decided that he wanted to go to *school* a school filled with *humans*. I had asked him why and he said he *liked* them and wanted *friends*."

"So what did you do? Did you let him go?"

"Oh yeah, I let him go. I signed him up and brought him there the first day. Then I went home, packed up some shit, and left." He stopped shaking and sighed, silence filled the room.

"You . . . left?" Tentatively, I pushed him for more.

"Yup, I left."

"Just like that?"

"Sure. I figure that I was almost twice the age of going out on my own and he was already thirteen. Even for being part human he could take care of himself. Your parents left you when you were thirteen."

"I had my aunt to help me though."

"Well I wasn't exactly thinking straight. I honestly didn't care if he lived or died. Anyway only vampires with families normally stayed in one place for that long, and we were *far* from a family." More silence followed. He stared at the ceiling after that.

"He hates me now. Wants to kill me."

"Well why's that? He did sort of kill your parents indirectly, why does he hate *you*?" He wanted to tell me, I just knew it.

"I left him a note, explaining everything. How our mom cheated on my dad and how he was born. He knew he was half vampire by then, naturally. I told him and taught him how to hunt, though he felt bad about it, he did it regardless."

"So he wants to kill you over a note and for telling him who his dad was or whatever?"

"No not exactly. I told him it was his fault our mom and his pseudo-dad killed each other, except I said it a little harsher than that. I wasn't nice to him and just shit built up over the years. On top of how much we didn't like each other already, it sort of worked out like that. He isn't emotionally stable either way so he was bound to go crazy at some point."

"Oh. So am I to assume that your brother-"

"Half brother."

"Okay, half brother. He found you today or ran into you and you guys got in a fight?"

"Yeah pretty much. He's been following me since I left him, finding me and trying to ruin my life pretty much."

"How?"

"If he sees that I've made friends or something he'll try to kill them or make them kill me, or something of that nature. It's a hindrance. So yes, he found me again which means he's going to go after you or make you go after me or I don't know."

I lightly touched his bruise and he flinched just the slightest bit, "Did you win the fight?"

"Yes, I always do. I'm older, a better fighter, and he's only half vampire."

"You didn't kill him, did you?" The thought of him getting violent enough to kill scared me.

"No, not this time, I'm planning on waiting until it's an even fight."

"Well that's . . . noble I guess the word is." At least he wasn't an unfair fighter I suppose. It really could be worse.

"So what's your brother name, and what does he look like? So I know who he is when he tries to kill me."

"I won't let that happen, I doubt he'd kill a girl anyway. But he'll tell you lies, they're very believable too, so watch out. He's got black hair and stands out pretty well. Not exactly the most subtle kid out there."

The feeling of cold dread seeped into my bones.

Because that sounds like somebody I already met. But it couldn't be. No, Zeek wasn't half vampire, he wasn't Chase's half brother, he was just some kid I met a few times.

Who already knows and hates Chase.

"Chase . . . what's his name?" He took a deep breath and tried to recompose himself, since he looks out of sorts again.

"Zeek. That little bastards name is Zeek."

. . .

Awh, shit.

12

Feral Danger

I loved you like I knew you,
And you took it all away,
I loved you like I knew you,
And you faked it just for play.
-Nicole Evans

"Chase, Zeek knows where I live." *How mad is he going to be? I didn't know though. Probably shouldn't have let a stranger in my house and all but I didn't think he was dangerous . . . Chase should have warned me about something as important as this, I would have kept a lookout.*

"It's okay, Wynter, let's not get ahead of ourselves. We have no reason to think that. I doubt he does just yet."

"But Chase, he really does."

"Wynter, I've only seen him once since I've been with you so I highly doubt that he knows where you live already."

"Chase," taking a deep breath, I spit it out, "I know Zeek. I met him on my bus when his motorcycle broke down. We've talked." Chases eyes widened and he stood up fast in front of where I sat on the couch. I said the last part really fast, to get it over with quickly,

"He'sgivenmearidehomebeforeandIlethiminside."

"Shit, Wynter!!" Chase kneeled with one knee on the edge of the couch; one leg extended to the floor. He slammed his hands on the couch as well, on either side of my head.

"Shit, *Wynter*? Shit, Chase! What the hell was that, you could have hit me in the face!" I pushed his chest to get out of this new imprisonment but he wouldn't budge. I sank into the cushions and looked up at him. He had this wild look in his eye, almost feral. His teeth were showing, lips pulled back, and he was looking at me like a starving wolf would a deer.

"Chase? Chase? Don't be mad, please? Don't look at me like that, I didn't mean to." He said nothing. His silence and stare of impending doom was frightening me. I didn't think it was scary at first but just having him stare at me like that, it was bone chilling.

His eyes shook and he was trembling with anger. His brown hair was moved from its normal place in his eyes and I got the full effect of his rage.

"Tell me everything you two talked about. Right now." Never before had I see this side of Chase. I didn't like it. Normally I would have a flippant remark or something, I don't put up with being told what to do like that, but he had on such a look I think he would slit my throat if I didn't comply.

"C-Chase? Is he going to kill me?" He moved his left hand to the side of my face and gripped my cheek. His hand was shaking like he was trying to control his anger, it hurt. I pulled at it with my own hand but the grip on my cheek was too strong.

Is he this mad?! He's never hurt me before, what is this? I looked up at him but he wasn't looking back, just through me. It wasn't intentional, Chase was paralyzed with anger, as I now was in fear; I let my hand trying to stop him drop.

"Chase, lemme go! Ouch, *Chase*!" The pain wasn't unbearable, but it was far from pleasant. I slapped his hand one more time as a last ditch effort to make him let go and come back to me.

"Chase let me go you're hurting me!!" He was still trying to control himself, "Chase! I said, *let me go dammit*!"

Chase was shaking and he looked like he was going crazy. So naturally I did what any other scared girl in pain would. I slapped the bastard clean across the face.

"Get a hold of yourself, Chase!" His eyes stopped going out of control and he immediately dropped his hand, looking at it like it was a piece of trash.

"Wynter . . . oh shit Wynter." He lifted his hands and started putting them onto my face again; but I flinched and he pulled back.

"Wynter I'm so sorry, I didn't mean to hurt you. I-I just couldn't control myself I wasn't trying to hurt you I was trying to," he lifted his hands, hesitated, then put them on my face, wiping away tears I didn't know had come, "I was trying to hold onto something to control myself I was, I was trying to control myself . . ."

Sniffing, I held onto his wrists, "It's okay, Chase, I know you weren't trying to. You were mad."

"That's no excuse, don't forgive me, that was awful. Disgusting. I swore I would never let myself lose control and scare you. Here I am losing control, scaring you and *hurting* you. I'm so sorry Wynter, I love you I would never do it intentionally."

"I love *you* Chase, I know you, I know you wouldn't." I gave him a kiss to show I believed him.

What is he to me? Is he my boyfriend? Can I even do that?

"You just finished telling me," I ended the kiss as well; but he was still upset, "that Zeek has hurt people before and I go and tell you that I've let him inside. I understand, I mean you were worried about me, he could hurt me like he hurt the others."

He told me Zeek has found all his friends from the past; he was mad. I know he didn't do it on purpose. I could become like one of the others. Wait . . . that doesn't make sense. If Chase left Zeek at fifteen, how many times could that have happened before? I've known him for just about four years . . .

"Chase, you told me that he finds you and ruins friendships or something and has even gone as far as to kill people close to you, right?" I wiped the rest of my runaway tears, that's embarrassing.

"Yes, but I won't let him get to you." He was checking out my cheek. It still stung and would probably bruise but I wasn't going to tell him that.

"Chase, how is that possible?"

"What do you mean?" He froze and looked at me weirdly.

"You just told me you left him when you were fifteen. You have been my friend or whatever we are now since you were like fifteen or sixteen, how has that happened to you before, then?" Chase looked like I was an adult catching him with his hand in the cookie jar. His coal eyes flashed and snapped back and forth in their sockets.

"I, um, yes I said that. My bad." He looked like he was sorting through some things in his mind.

"What do you mean your bad? You told me you're nineteen, you are, right? So that only gives him like a year at the absolute most to do that to you. You implied it had happened a lot of times." He didn't make any sense. Chase looked around, lost.

"Yeah, I guess I exaggerated, but only a little."

"Oh, please. That's the best you've got? What do you mean by 'a little'?"

"Well, he has yet to find or kill anyone . . ."

"Chase! So, what? That story you just told me was only that? A story to scare me into hating your brother too?" This is infuriating; I wish I hadn't invited him over today. Such drama, and from a *guy* especially.

"No, everything besides that was true. But it's what he promised to do. He might as well have. He killed any chances I've had to make friends or settle down, I didn't want anyone to get hurt so I never stayed in one place."

"But you've stayed here. You don't care if I get hurt then?"

"I do, Wynter, I care so much. I wouldn't be able to stand it if you were hurt, that's why this," He kissed my cheek, "Makes me want to die. I wouldn't be able to let someone who hurt you live, but here I am hurting you."

I grabbed onto his hand and held it tight, "I told you that I understood, you didn't mean to!"

"And I told you not to forgive me, if you won't punish me by being mad, it's going to eat away at me."

"It's just a little red, if that, you don't need to feel so bad about it."

"*Please* Wynter just pretend?"

"Okay, okay, fine. Chase you hurt me for absolutely no reason and now I'm really mad at you and I will be forever." I crossed my arms in mock anger. He sat down and just shook his head.

"The point is, Wynter, that I never did settle. When I did here I had no intentions of talking to people, I still almost never go into the town. I didn't want to do anything but eat and survive until I could finally live knowing that Zeek was gone."

"What happened to that plan? Where do you sleep anyway? Where do you keep your clothes? What about food? Where do you get that? 'Cause I know you eat in-between your *other* meals."

"You happened to that plan!" he shouted, "I was just hanging out at a nice pond I had found and here comes this chick out of nowhere. Trust me when I tell you that it was a mistake, befriend you, loving you, but one I would repeat over and over again."

"Well I don't think it was a mistake. I think we were supposed to meet. So there."

"No, not a mistake like I regret it now, but a mistake like I was suppose to be more aware, to not let anyone find me. I blew that."

"I'm glad you did." Smiling, I looked up at him and snuggled against his side. A long arm wrapped around me, pulling me closer.

"Me too. As for the other questions you have; I sleep wherever I can. When I started living around here I would use houses if residents were on vacation or something. But then I almost got caught, had to jump out a window, so I went and got a tent. That's where I keep my clothes."

"A tent? Man that must be awful when it gets cold! What have you been doing in the winter?"

"It's actually not bad at all, I got a nice one. But to tell you the truth I haven't had many instances where I've had to sleep outside in the winter."

"Well where do you go then?"

"We met before the first winter I had on my own . . . I sort of took some space in your garage when I heard it was going to snow, or when there was snow on the ground . . ."

It took a few seconds to sink in. Who would have thought that Chase was in my house and had been for years? We had sleepovers and I didn't even know about it!

"You mad?" He gave me an innocent look, he knew I wasn't.

"No, in fact it doesn't even surprise me all that much, to tell you the truth. But where did all the money come from? For the tent, your clothes, your food?"

"Well I had some money left over from when I was with my parents. We didn't have much because we made just enough to cover the bills and small things. I got a job to support Zeek and a small apartment when I was still looking after him."

"Nobody questioned a young kid looking after another younger one with no parents?"

"It was one of those sketchy parts of a town. As long as we paid and nothing got badly damaged they didn't give a damn."

"Sounds like a good way to raise a kid brother."

"I couldn't do any better, and if I could I don't think that he deserved better."

"I guess you're right." Chase patted my arm, to signify that I needed to be fair and understand. I squeezed his hand in reply.

"I had clothes from when we were a family, I got a few more things with the money that was left. As for food, well I stole a lot of it. I don't need to eat, really. I mean it tastes good and I crave some of it sometimes, but I don't need it to survive."

"Where'd you steal it from?"

"Supermarkets, small stores, the houses I stayed in for a while. When I met you, though, and we hung out, you always offered some, so I didn't need to. Speaking of which, where do you get *your* food? No job no money no food, Wynter."

"My aunt. I send her a list through email and she orders it and has it sent through this store that delivers."

He gave me a look.

"Hey, it's part of her job as my guardian!"

"You are such a lazy ass," he said.

I hit him.

13

Chase's Trip

Scream as the cold pain needles you,
After the initial contact, it burns.
Love, once so strong and pure, now tainted.
My lungs collapse, bathed in ice water.
-Nicole Evans

Every good feeling I've ever felt before swirled around my head and I held on to him tighter. I gripped his hair and opened my eyes for a split second. The world was an array of neon colors, dancing together. I felt a prick as his fangs dove deeper into my skin, fighting for the last drop he could take. My chest was pressed flush against his and I was holding on for dear life.

Once again, all too soon, I felt Chase slow down and pull his mouth away from me. A trickle of blood seeped from the new wound on my neck and I felt him lick it away. He repeated this, kissing my neck until there was nothing left and the two punctures were clean. I let his hair go from my hold on it.

"Enough?" I whispered, faintly. I was getting better at giving so much blood, but it still effected me.

"You wish it wasn't."

"Shut up, Chase, you do too." He smirked and kissed me; I tasted the faint taste of my blood on his lips. I don't know how he liked it; I broke the kiss because the taste was ruining it.

He touched the spot on my neck, it was sore and sensitive already, it would be for a while.

"You seem to be doing better, Wynter, didn't faint or anything this time."

What he said was true, I *was* getting better. I remember the first time I flat out fainted after giving so much blood to him. It's been weeks since then, and every weekend it was the same thing. We would meet up somewhere and he would bite me.

Our Saturdays together were my favorite part of the week; I looked forward to it every single day. I learned how to take care of myself more so I could be stronger so that I could give more blood without so much of a reaction after the fact.

Chase ran his finger over the marks one last time and moved up, resting his hand on my cheek. The memory of when he lost control and hurt me burned in my mind. It had been so scary and even now, weeks later; I woke up in the middle of the night, terrified.

His face, his eyes, everything about him was such raw anger. The look he gave me and how he couldn't regain control, it was still with me. But he didn't know that, and I wasn't going to tell him and make him feel guilty. Especially since he's so sweet to me all the time.

"I love you Wynter." I kissed him in reply, a long, lasting kiss.

"I love you too Chase, I will always love you." He smirked like there was a joke I wasn't getting and whispered, "I know" into my ear. Hot breath tickled my face and I giggled.

"Stop it, Chase you know that tickles."

"Oh it does? Really?" He moved his hands to my ribs and gave a little squeeze.

"How about that Wynter? Does that tickle?" I grabbed his hands and tried to push them away.

"If you dare I'm seriously going to *kill* you!" His hands weren't moving any more but just having them there was enough to kill me.

"I'm not gonna, I just have the potential to!" He rubbed my ribs and I started squealing.

"Chase I'm going to kill you, I'm going to kill you! I don't care, you're gonna do it, it's not just the potential, I know you will!!" I was twisting trying to get out of his grip but since I was standing against him it was hard to. The more he rubbed his hands on my ribs, the more I thought he was going to tickle me and the more I moved, making it worse.

"Wynter I'm not doing anything, you're the one whose moving and making it tickle!"

"Shut up and stop Chase I know you're having a lot of fun watching me be in tickle pain or whatever it's called!"

"I really am but once again, I am doing absolutely *nothing!*"

"Gaaaah! *Stop it, stop it, stop it I'm going to diiiiiiie!*" I was screaming and moving like someone had lit me on fire. He always does this. 'Oh it's just the potential, I wouldn't really tickle you!' is what he says. But every time he may as well because I freak out like this and it tickles anyway!

I grabbed his ribs too and tried to tickle him, all it made him do was squirm around a little. How is it that guys aren't nearly as ticklish as girls are?

"Oh, that's it Wynter! I told you I wasn't going to tickle you but this means war!"

"Crap, no Chase, *no*!" But it was too late; he had already started tickling me. All I can do is laugh and move around trying to get his fingers away from my waist.

He pushed me against a tree right near the pond and went all out. Moving so fast, cheating with vampire skills, from my waist and ribs to my neck and my arms, I was laughing so hard I pretty much started crying.

"Stop-it-I-will-kill-you." I couldn't breath and he stopped, laughing at me like a madman.

"You should see your face Wynter you're crying!"

"Ha-ha very funny! Loser, my ribs are falling off!"

"Oh no, I'll hold them in then!" He put his hands back where he had the damned potential again and started rubbing my sore rib cage.

"If you don't stop I will rip your arms off Chase, and that's a promise."

"Stopping."

He looked at me and I looked at him, smiling from ear to ear.

I love him so much.

"I love you too Wynter, always keep that in mind, alright?"

"I didn't say I love you, so you can't say that you love me too Chase."

"You're looking at me like you're thinking it, so that's good enough in my book. You were thinking it, were you not?"

"Shut up." I grabbed him and kissed him, feeling his smirk as I did so. He was trying to break away to say more, so I pressed my lips harder against his.

He grabbed me and pulled me closer, letting his words go and falling into our kiss. We started out with me trying to shut him up and soon there was a full-blown make-out session. He grabbed my butt and I smiled into the kiss, I knew he would do that. The kisses became fierce as he pulled me even closer to him than I already was.

"You're an inappropriate kid. Just plain disgusting, I can't believe you." I joked once we had broke apart some time later.

"You started it."

"In my defense you wouldn't stop talking. You weren't exactly trying to stop me though, were you?"

"I plead the fifth."

"Yeah, you would."

"Let's go back to your house, sound good? It's getting cold, I heard it's gonna snow soon."

"Yeah I heard that too. I guess we should be expecting it, we are in December after all."

Wow this year has been just flying by . . .

~ ~ ~ ~ ~

Back at my house we started to make hot chocolate. I got the mugs, spoons, and chocolate. I mixed everything together and put milk in the bottom of the mug so it wouldn't be too hot. Then I put everything away. Chase boiled water.

"I'm glad you're so helpful there, bud."

"Just doing my part to make this easier on you there, Wynter. No need to thank me."

I laughed, "No worries there."

Sitting down with our mugs I noticed the lack of marshmallows. No cup of hot chocolate is complete without those.

"Chase, can you go get the marshmallows?"

"Where are they?"

"Oh I dunno, probably in the pantry unless I are them all again. That's actually pretty possible."

He got up and went around the corner to look for them, there's a rustling noise and things are being thrown all about, and he came back empty handed.

"Sorry, none left. You ate them for breakfast or lunch at school I'll be willing to bet."

"No! What a tragedy! No marshmallows in my hot chocolate! Doom, doom, dooooom! Could life get any worse?"

I slammed my head on the table and I could just picture Chase wincing next to me. Feeling his hand pat my back, I turned my head to look at him. He looked quite uncomfortable.

"Don't worry, it didn't hurt."

"No, not that, though that too. Really Wynter stop banging your head on tables every time you run out of something, it isn't healthy."

"But my marshiemellows are gone . . ."

"And there will be other ones."

"Fine. What's eating you then?"

"I have some sorta bad news. Well not really bad so much as it might annoy you. It's going to bother me to a certain extent too, but I have to. Well not so much have to as should since I have every year before this-"

"Chase, I don't need a lengthy explanation, just tell me what's wrong."

"I'm going to go visit my parent's grave. I have been once a year every years since they . . . passed on."

"Why would I be mad at you for that? If my parents were dead I would do the same thing."

"Well they're pretty far away."

"Like how far?" My stomach dropped. How long would I have to be without him?

"A few days. A day each way roughly and I'll spend a day there most likely."

"Oh, well that's okay. It's only three days. You wouldn't take any longer, would you?"

"No, if anything it will be less time. I figure it would be faster by car but since I don't have one and neither do you I'll be riding on buses the way there and back."

"Oh man that sucks. Will you be okay on a bus? I bet we could get someone to drive you? Maybe?" But we both know that wasn't possible.

"It's a pretty short ride, just longer with the stops. I'll try and make it two days, maybe a little more. You gonna be okay here by yourself?"

"Yeah, not a problem, I'll just miss you is all. But I don't want to sound self-centered. When do you leave?"

"I thought I would early tomorrow morning. That way I can spend the rest of the Saturday with you and leave Sunday. I'll be back Tuesday night at the absolute latest."

"Oh. I like the early warning there, jerk!" I shoved him sarcastically.

"If I had told you earlier then you would have just been upset the whole time before I left!"

"True. Well you can stay with me for today then and will I see you in the morning? Probably not, since you said the bus leaves early."

"Yeah, most likely not, unless you want to wake up at five thirty?"

"No freaking thank you!"

"Not even for me? Wynter, I'm crushed!" Chase put his hand over his heart as if it were breaking.

"Don't try and guilt me into it! Anyway, I think you'll live, you're coming back Tuesday."

"That's my line."

"Well I stole it! Um, by the way, is there any way that I can go with you Chase?" I gave my best 'challenged' puppy dog look, to make him laugh and maybe say yes.

"No way Wynter, you need to stay in school and actually apply yourself. No skipping more than you normally do already."

"No fair. I'm not going to be able to concentrate if you're away anyway. Doesn't make sense for me to go when I can be with you visiting your parents!"

"It's not just that though Wynter. Don't take this the wrong way but it's sort of something that I like to do on my own, you know what I mean?"

"Yeah, sorry, I get it. I would feel the same way if I were you."

"Thanks, plus you need to do something school-wise."

"I hate you."

He kissed me to make it better.

~~~~~

The rest of the day went nicely, but I felt bad because I knew tomorrow that I wasn't going to be able to see him for a few days. At eleven-ish Chase woke me up; I fell asleep next to him while we were watching a movie.

"Wynter, I have to go, okay? Gotta pack up some stuff and find out exactly when the bus is going to be leaving."

"Alright, I'll see you Tuesday then."

"I love you Wyn."

"I love you too Chase. Have a safe trip thing! Tell your parents that I say hi, okay?"

"Will do." He left me with a kiss and a promise to be back as soon as possible.

14

Zeek's Anger

You're a gasoline rainbow,
So toxic and so alluring.
A mistake looked down upon,
Created by chance.
-Nicole Evans

"I love you, I'll see you in a few days." Chase kissed the top of my head and began walking away. Meaning to get up, I stirred, but it was just too early.

"Mhnh." I heard a chuckle and then he was gone out the door he came in.

~ ~ ~ ~ ~

I whined into the phone, "Sundays are as boring as hell."

"It's not even noon and you're already bored? Do something around the house!"

"I just pierced my lip again, now there isn't anything else *to* do!"

"Why'd you wait so long since the last one?"

"I wanted to make sure the other was healed before I did another, and I couldn't decide between snake bites or spider bites."

"What did you end up doing?"

"I went with spider bites, it was more 'me' if you know what I mean." *Really I didn't want to be reminded of* his *snakebites every time I looked in the mirror . . . the bastard that hurt Chase.*

"Randomly choose today?"

"I don't know, for some reason it seemed just like the right day to do it. Just a feeling I guess."

"Well in that case why don't we do something together? To celebrate? Really I'm just looking for an excuse to hang out with you."

I spoke into the phone, "I'll rephrase that last statement about being bored as hell: I'm as lazy as hell too."

"Oh Wynter, what am I going to do with you?" Zelena sighed dramatically.

"I dunno, put me down while I still have my dignity?"

"You lost that when you became a stalker."

"I'm no stalker!!" I screeched.

"Speaking of which, where's Chase? Normally you wouldn't be calling me 'cause you'd be too busy with him."

"He's on a trip."

"Where?" *Am I allowed to tell her? No, I wouldn't want Chase to tell someone if I were in his position . . .*

"I think he said something about seeing some old friends?" I flopped down on my back in my room; Zelena was going to see right through that.

Actually believing the lie, "Oh, that sounds like fun, maybe while he's doing that you can catch up with one of *your* old friends!"

"Hm, I don't think I know of anyone that I would want to hang out with . . ."

"You're not very nice, are you?"

"Not really, but that's why you accept me. You want me on your side in case I snap, right?"

"But of course; always befriend the crazy kids, that way you aren't one of the ones shot."

"Now you're the one not being very nice." We both laughed.

Continuing I told her, "Well if I *have* to hang out with someone it might as well be you. Wanna go somewhere?"

"Yeah. Shopping or something?" I got off my bed and paced around the room.

"Sounds good, we can go out to lunch too. I think I have enough of my monthly allowance from Aunt Emily to get something this time."

There was a crash downstairs; *Nightmare must be after the fish again. She'll never learn that he's in glass. Poor Sharkbait must be scared out of his little fishy mind.*

"Meow?" Nightmare brushed and bumped against my leg, asking to be picked up.

"Oh little Nightmare," I picked her up.

Zelena's voice through the phone asked, "So when can you come over? I'll drive." Yeah, she could stupid drive with her stupid car.

If Nightmare is up here, then what knocked something over downstairs? Paranoia and my love for the supernatural spoke up in my mind and I tip toed over to the hall near the stairs.

"Wynter? When do you want to come over?" Zelena's voice asked again. Her normal sounding voice was dimming the thrill of expecting something to happen.

I always assume that there are ghosts in my house when I hear a noise, just another part of me that weird others out; I watch and read too much in the horror genre.

"I don't know, I'll start getting my shoes on-"

"So like three hours?" She likes to make fun of my boots, since they go up to my knees.

"Funny girl, it shouldn't be too long."

"Wynter, why are you whispering? I can't hear you." She said, I didn't even realize that I had been.

I turned away from the stairs and responded, "I just heard a crash downstairs. It wasn't Nightmare, I'm going to go check it out."

"And it'll end up being something stupid, just like every time. You're paranoid."

"Shh! You'll give away my position! And no I'm not, I want to see a ghost is all!"

"Fine, you're not paranoid you're freaking insane." But she shut up anyway.

After I start thinking about ghosts or whatever I turn finding the source of the noise they made into a mission.

"I'll just stay on the line while you hunt down the wind then."

One of these days there's going to actually be something here. I have ghosts in my house, I know it. They can't hide forever, I'm gonna see one eventually!

Singing "Prisoner" by Jeffree Star in my head I pretended to be a secret agent on a mission, not sure how the song related to a secret agent, but it worked for me. I got downstairs before Zelena's patience was up.

"You done yet?"

"I said to be quiet! What if there actually *is* something down here this time? I heard a noise. Don't talk I don't wanna scare it away!" I hissed into the receiver.

I peeked around the corner into the never used dining room and jumped out from where I had been hiding,

"*Hah!*" I looked around, pointing my finger in every direction, trying to find the cultrate.

"Anyone there?"

I sighed in disappointment, "Screw you, Zelena, you believe in ghosts too."

"I believe in spirits, the kind that go directly to Heaven." She corrected me.

"Tomato tomahto."

"So anyway," She went on, "If you're done with the ghost hunt for now, when you coming over?"

"Stay on the phone and I'll get my shoes from outside, they had some mud on them from the woods."

I walked normally, forsaking the tiptoeing until next time, and went to open the door. Reaching for the knob, it started tuning on its own.

Stepping back, "What the hell?"

Zelena asked me what I meant by that through the phone, but I couldn't respond because after I backed up, Zeek walked right into my house uninvited.

"What are you doing here?"

"What are you talking about, Wynter??" Zelena yelled into the phone, which I brought to my face; not taking my eyes off of Zeek for a second, and responded,

"I can't hang out after all Lena, sorry. Talk to you later." Before she could respond I had hit the end button and put the phone back in my pocket.

"What the hell are you doing here?" I automatically pulled my hair over my shoulder, to cover the mark on my neck from yesterday as to avoid another breakdown like the one he had so many weeks ago.

"I haven't seen you in a long time, this is how you greet me?" His words were playful but his voice suggested a serious business.

"Yeah, it is. I can greet you however I want to since I found out you're a crazy bastard."

"I did just try to sneak in through your kitchen window before I tried the door. Unlocked by the way, not too smart. So I guess you're right; I am a crazy bastard."

"You what!? Get out right now Zeek, I swear to God I'll-"

He cut me off, "You'll what? Hit me? You've got to be five foot five at the tallest, I'm five foot ten, I have a whole head on you."

"So since I can't hit you, you'll hit me? You gonna kill me like you told Chase you would? Get out of my house *right now Zeek*!"

Instead he took another step in, shutting the door behind him, and locking it.

"I'm not going anywhere, neither are you," That explains locking it, harder for me to run out, "We've got to talk about him. I didn't come over sooner than today because I thought I scared you last time we talked."

"Talked? You stole my towel then went ape shit! *Then* you got in a fight with Chase! I don't even know you that well and you're acting like you know everything about me!"

I walked into the kitchen to find a broken glass on the ground; the window he tried to open must have hit it. That explains the 'ghost' noise.

"I'm sorry Wynter but if you knew what was happening, you'd realize how called for that was!"

I ignored him and picked up the big pieces of glass from the linoleum, placing them on the counter.

"Get out, I don't care how tall you are, I'll stab you or something. I'll fight dirty, you don't deserve a fair one."

He ignored my threat, "You went with spider bites instead."

"Yeah, okay, change the subject why don't you. Let's ignore everything and talk about my new piercing. Yes, I did it this morning actually. I was trying to avoid thinking about you by getting a different one from you. Anything else you want to add?"

"You think of me? Why Wynter, I'm touched!"

"I think about you and how much I hate you for what you did to Chase!! Don't turn this into a joke, it's far from it."

He looked down dejectedly, "Yeah, I guess you're right, but I can't talk to you if you're just gonna piss off at me the whole time."

"I have no intention of talking to you anyway, hence why I want you out. Preferably now as opposed to later."

"I'm not leaving." I walked over to the knife drawer and pulled out the biggest one I had.

"I will cut your arms off."

"Do it. I'll still have my legs to keep me here and my mouth to talk to you."

"Zeek," I took what I hoped was a menacing step towards him, "I liked you, thought you could be a good friend. But Chase told me who you are, what you did to him and what you've threatened to do."

"I'm not going to hurt you, Wynter, I would never, could never." He took a step closer with his arms outstretched; I took a half step back.

"If you get any closer I'll cut you, I promise I'll do it. I'm not stupid, Zeek, you're trying the whole 'being nice to make me lower my guard and then kill' thing. I've seen it in movies a hundred times."

"That's twisted."

"*You're* twisted. I saw Chase's face after the two of you fought."

I backed into the living room so that in the event he came after me, there would at least be a couch and coffee table between us. He may be taller but I could jump over them faster to get away. *I hope.*

"So I guess Chase went with the story that I'm his half brother. Am I right?" He stepped, carefully, towards the living room with me. I was in front of the couch and he was behind it. I still held the knife in front of my body.

"Story? There's no story, he told me the truth about how your mom cheated on his dad and you were born. And if you don't think I'm serious about taking a swipe at you, you're dead wrong. I know it'll hurt you, Chase told me everything about vampires so I know it would hurt even them. You're only *half* vampire, you won't heal as fast."

"*I am not half vampire and I am not related to that bag of shit!*" He screamed.

I screamed back with just as much intensity, "You are so and you told Chase you would kill anyone who he got close to, I'm close to him, we love each other! I'm not letting you kill me, get out of my house we're done talking about it!!"

"C'mere Wynter, he's lied to you through his teeth, you've got to at least listen to me!" He started to run around the side to get to me.

"Get the hell away!" I jumped on the couch, knife still in hand, and tried to jump to the other side; But Zeek was faster than I thought he would be and he grabbed me before I could get to the other side.

"Ouch, Zeek you're hurting me!" I was on my back on the couch and he was sitting on top of me.

"Are you gonna listen now?"

Have to think fast. What will get him off??

Thinking quickly, "Ouch! Ow, ow Zeek, the knife!" I howled bloody murder and his eyes went wide instantly, "Oh God ow, Zeek *the knife!*"

"Holy shit Wynter, I didn't mean to, I'm sorry!" He got off of my stomach fast as he could. The knife that had been laying harmlessly, thank God, under my back was now in my hand. I tried again to jump over the couch and get away from him, trying to put the element of surprise I had, to use.

"Wha-?? Wynter!" Zeek, who had been on the floor in horror at the thought I had been stabbed, quickly regained composure and went after me again.

Almost made it this time, but Zeek took hold of my waist and dragged me down again. This time I felt the knife slice my wrist as he threw it away from us.

"Ow, dammit!"

"You're not tricking me this time, Wynter." He was on top of me again, sitting on my stomach and holding my wrists so I couldn't claw him, which I was planning on doing.

"No, for real, when you threw it, the thing cut me. Look at my wrist." He lifted his hand a little, not must, in case it was a trick probably, and saw I wasn't lying this time.

"Crap, well it's your fault. It's a small cut, you'll be okay. I wouldn't have thrown it if you hadn't gotten it."

"Well I wouldn't have gotten it if you had just left."

"Well I would have left if you would just talk to me for a second."

"Well I would have talked to you if I didn't know that you were a crazy guy."

"I am not crazy."

"You tried to get in through my kitchen window and normally that makes someone look quite craz-" the feeling of Zeek's lips on my own cut me off. It was a shut-up-right-now-you're-ranting sort of kiss.

"Met mur mips mohff of meph!" I tried to scream but he wasn't budging.

Breaking away for a split second he replied,

"I'm not moving them until you agree to talk to me Wynter. Plain and simple." He replaced his lips on my own, one of his snakebites clipped against my own spider bites. I didn't want to give in but he was getting pushy with his tongue. *Such a boy.*

"Mokay! Jest met moff!" *He destroyed Chase's family, his life, and he's kissing me, again.*

After I was freed, "I told you not to do that last time you did."

"You wouldn't shut up. Are you going to listen now?"

"For a little, just cause I know you won't leave me alone until I do. Not because I trust or will believe you. I'm getting a bandage first."

I walked to the bathroom, alone; he was giving me some room. The cut looked worst than it was, but without ointment, there would be an infection. After dealing with that, I went and sat down on the opposite side of the couch from Zeek. He licked his lips, teasing me.

"Screw you."

"You wish."

"Not on your life, trust me." I rolled my eyes. I hate him, hate him, hate him for what he did; but at the same time . . . well he's making it hard to.

"You'll take that back when you learn about all the lies Chase has told you."

"We'll see. Start talking so you can leave faster."

"The first lie; Chase is not my half brother. I would kill myself if he were, after killing him that is. That's probably the only truth he's told you, by the way, that I want to kill him."

"But why? I don't believe that you two aren't brothers, yet, but why do you want to kill him so badly? If it has nothing to do with family, then why?"

"It actually has everything to do with family. The reason that I want to kill Chase is for revenge." He took a deep breath, all the former playfulness had since drained from his eyes.

Edging him on, "Why do you want revenge on him, Zeek?"

"He killed my sister. He took her life and for that I've promised to take his."

15

No Such Thing as Coincidences

Toxic, poison, you're polluted.
But so bright, you're so bright.
I can't help but stare,
And the world walks by.
-Nicole Evans

"He did not."

"You haven't even let me start Wynter."

"Don't if you're going to start like that. Chase has never killed anyone human or anyone innocent, he told me so. If you're going to force me to listen to some bull story then at least start with something believable." I crossed my arms, pissed off already. But if it'll make him leave, then I can take a little of it I guess.

"Whatever. Let me start with the real," he said real while doing that quotation gesture that annoys everyone, "story then."

"Oh please do."

"I'm going to tell you the short version in that case. I don't remember or know every detail anyway."

"As long as it's over soon." He rolled his eyes, annoyed with my negativity. But I was annoyed with his lies, so we're even.

"My sister was eighteen when she met Chase. Back then his name was Scott, he claimed to be twenty-"

I interrupted, repulsed at how this was going, "Zeek, *Chase* has never-"

"Wynter, let me tell the story then I'll leave. You can believe it, you can ignore it, but let me tell it and then I'm gone." I curtly nodded once, I could do that; *not* believe it, I mean.

"As I was saying, she met him at eighteen and he was twenty. We lived in Chinook, Montana if you want to know, which I doubt that you did."

"I don't care." He was losing what little charm he had left with this story.

"Wynter, try to understand, by the end of this story, you may see him in a totally different light."

"Whatever."

Sighing, "I think she was one of his first victims," he cringed, "he wasn't very good compared to how he is now. But he was good enough, I guess." Zeek looked hard at his hands, like it was hard to get out. Lies don't come naturally to him I guess.

"Her name was Kaylee, I looked up to her my whole life. She was three years older than me, so I was fifteen when Scott/Chase killed her." He looked me in the eyes, "You're a special case, Wynter. Never before you has he spent so long on someone. It's always been a year, two tops, since I've known him; you've been with him for what, four years or something? It took my sister six months, though she always did fall for people really quickly . . ."

"If this was true, which it isn't, but if it was, why would he stay with me for so long?" Zeek gave me a look, like he knew what I was thinking, but he didn't; I'm just curious as to how in depth he would take this lying.

"I have no idea, but it can't be a good thing. I don't know exactly what happened between them, I mean she was older than me. I was just a little brother, she wasn't going to share anything about her love life with a kid."

"You don't look like you're fifteen." *Ahah! Caught him in a lie. That was too easy.*

"I'm not anymore. This wasn't recent Wynter, it happened a long, *long*, time ago."

"Well how old are you, how long ago *was* it?"

"Just listen. I wasn't supposed to ever meet him, he didn't want see me, but I did, just once. It was a surprise visit; I was at a friend's house and came home early to see him leaving. The look I got, it looked like he wanted to kill me."

Weird how the story Chase, Scott I guess, didn't want to meet Zeek. Just like how Chase, my real Chase, didn't want to meet Zelena . . .

"He led her on, filling her head with lies about true love, everlasting love. I didn't hear much about him but I would eavesdrop once in a while when she talked with her friends."

"Not very polite."

"*You're* the one with the attitude right now so I wouldn't be talking." His cold words snapped at me and I backed off.

I flinched, "Touchy little guy aren't you?"

He pointedly ignored me, "Scott turned Kaylee into a blood bride; I watched him do it. He took her out by the woods behind out house. At the time I had no idea what was going on, but now I do, and I wish every day that I had stopped him."

"There isn't anything wrong with being a blood bride, Zeek. Or giving blood for that matter." His face paled and he angrily bit at his lip ring. I took smug satisfaction at how upset he was getting over my statement.

"There's plenty wrong with it, first off is that it just isn't *natural*. But had that been the only problem, it wouldn't have mattered. I would have been okay with her giving up her human life to spend a vampire life with the one she loved." He stared at the ceiling, then his hands. He looked like he had aged with telling the story.

"Scott turned her, then told her that she didn't deserve him."

"What?" Chase wouldn't do that to someone. Nobody could do that to someone, it just didn't happen.

"She begged, pleaded, groveled on the ground, for him to just take her as a servant. I couldn't move from where I was hidden. My sister was bleeding from her neck and begging to be a servant to a monster, it would have been pathetic had it not been so scary. There were no stages of grief for her, she accepted him leaving her in a nanosecond and went directly to degrading herself."

"She didn't even ask why?" *The story isn't true, the story isn't true . . . but it's interesting nonetheless.*

"No, and that still shocks me to this day. I know how much she loved him, how could she accept it so fast? She didn't let him explain, which pissed him off. I know because every single time he does it, explaining is his favorite part."

"Scott's evil." It's true; the boy from the story was evil.

"*Chase* is evil."

"They aren't the same person, Zeek, they couldn't be. I know Chase, maybe they look alike, but Scott and Chase aren't the same person."

He sighed again, one of those sighs that you hear before a person gives up on something; or in my case, someone.

Tentatively, because I didn't want him to think that I believed the lie, I asked, "What happened to her?"

A second later, "He killed her. Scott killed her right there in front of me."

There was nothing I could say. The story was true, that much I could tell. Everything about it, I think. Except that it wasn't Chase, it was Scott that did it. I believe every word of it except that it *was. Not. Chase.*

"How?"

"He had started walking away when she begged on the ground for him to take her with him, and he turned back. My God you should have seen the look in her eyes. It was like Heaven had sent her an angel; I could see that from so far away, hidden, in the dark. Scott walked up to her and gripped her shoulders, dragging Kaylee to her feet."

His throat caught between an escaped sob and a cough, "H-he picked her up and stared her in the eyes, and she looked back, already his blood bride."

Just a part of Zeek's past, a bad encounter with another vampire, there are a lot of them out there, it happens.

"Scott, Chase, whoever, bit into her throat and ripped it open."

I could see it happening in my mind, I could *feel* it. Her emotions coursed through me, her blood was my blood, and her doom was my doom. I felt like it was happening to me, I got sucked into who she was.

~ ~ ~ ~ ~

Scott, who looked a lot like Chase, walked back to me, and I was so happy. So happy that I could still be useful to him, even if he wouldn't love me. He picked me up; his arms are so strong and sure, just like he's always been. My blonde hair—*My hair? Her hair?*—Whipped around, catching for a moment in his fingers.

"I don't care if you don't love me, because I love you and I want to help you no matter what." *Whose words were those? Hers. Her last ones.*

Scott said nothing, but then again we never expected him to. *We. I am she, and she is I. We love Scott, there is nothing else. No one else.*

His eyes, black as the deepest part of the ocean, smothered our own.

In our head, we chanted, *I love you, I love you, I love you, I love you, I love you, I love you, I love you, Scott.*

His fangs, still dripping red with our blood, and white with his venom, lowered to the left side of our neck, and we sighed.

We could feel them prick on the far side, but it was unusually placed. Higher up than where he normally bit us, and too far back. His teeth seeped into our skin, but it wasn't a good feeling, as it so often was. It hurt this time.

We tried to speak, tried to ask Scott what he was doing, but nothing came out. Not that we couldn't have, but there wasn't enough time. For right before we were going to ask him what he was doing, Scott ran his teeth, still in our skin, from one side of out throat to the other.

Half a second passed before we realized what had just happened, and the pain started. We were losing blood fast, the knives in his mouth had cut our jugular, and red was just pouring out. The pain was unbearable, but it wasn't as bad as what we saw next.

Scott stood in front of us, watching us hold our neck in place, trying to keep the blood in. He was watching us fall to the ground, and he watched our face contort in pain.

"I'll be seeing you Kaylee, take care!" His laughter echoed in our mind and the world was spinning so fast. The last thing we saw was a smaller figure jump from the bushes and go running after him. Then we died.

~ ~ ~ ~ ~

I snapped back into my own body, breathing heavy, tears in my eyes. Zeek's story had brought me into her body. I don't know if the experience is what actually happened, what was real, or something I had created my head. But it didn't matter, either way it was still terrifying.

"I ran after him. I couldn't move until my sister had already died. I was in shock, stunned, at what I had just seen. I ran after him as hard and as fast as I could, but I never caught up to him. I still haven't."

"You've been after Scott since then?"

"For fifty years, and I've watched him do the same thing that he did to my sister, to girls like you."

"H-how old *are* you Zeek?"

"I'm sixty-five, technically. But I stopped ageing at roughly," he looked down at himself, trying to get a guestimate, "probably twenty or something."

"You kissed me. I've been kissed by a sixty-five year old man!" *Ew.*

"I'm a blood groom, so I still have the body of a teenager, and the mind of one too, you're okay."

That's defiantly true, him having the mind of a teenager.

"How are you one? Why? And where's the vampire that changed you?"

"I'm one so that I can find and kill Scott. That's the only reason. I found another vampire, totally by chance, and once she heard my story, changed me."

"Who is she?"

"Does it matter? Her name was Dementia, I literally found her by a stroke of good luck and then we parted ways. Haven't seen her since."

"Did you have parents?"

He looked sad, "Yeah, we did. It must have been awful for them to find a dead daughter in the woods and a missing son. I never went back to them but I kept up with the newspapers around there. It was a small town with a lot of wild animals, so the police automatically assumed that a wild animal got her and dragged me off."

"You never went back? Did you not think of how they would feel?" It was harsher than I intended.

"No, I just knew that I needed to get Scott back. If I could go back in time, I would have done the same thing. Do you have a sister? A brother? No, you don't so you couldn't possibly understand how I felt then and how I feel now."

We sat in silence for a while; there wasn't anything appropriate that I could say to him. Until:

"So what's this got to do with Chase?"

He looked pissed off, "Wynter! It has *everything* to do with Chase! Scott is Chase, Chase is Scott! He changes his name with every new girl and he alters his looks to fit in with the year. He's been doing this for decades maybe centuries is my guess."

"Zeek, I believe you," the look in his eyes made me regret my wording, "I believe that you aren't Chase's half brother. I don't know exactly why he told me that story, but I believe that it isn't true." The initial look in his eye faded but there was still hope there.

"He probably doesn't know why you're following him, and just came up with that to explain it to both himself and me."

"No, it's the truth, everything I told you is the truth!" The hope he had left seemed to drain away.

"I believe that all of that happened to you, to your sister, I believe that you're a blood groom and that you want to kill Scott. Hell, after that story, I want him dead too."

"Thank you."

"*But* you've got the wrong guy," He tried interrupting me but I continued on, "You said that you've been following him around all these years. How come you never caught him?"

"Well once he left a girl I would lose him sometimes for a few months at a time. Then find him again and have to plan for the perfect moment."

"So you lost him. And previously you said that he changed both his name and how he looks sort of. Is it not possible for you to have seen Chase and mistaken him for Scott?"

"No, I would recognize him anywhere."

"I'm sorry, Zeek, but you're wrong. I really hope that you find Scott, but Chase is *not* him. Now please, go. Leave us alone and don't come back. You've already scared me and hurt him because you mistook him for someone else."

"Wynter I'm telling you that I didn't, I'm trying to warn you as to what's going to happen in the future."

"Nothing bad will happen. I love Chase and he loves me, he's always protected me and been nothing but good to me."

"You're wrong. Someday you'll see that." He got up from the couch and I followed him to the door. He unlocked it and let himself out.

Pausing in the doorway, "Would you become his blood bride if he asked you to be?"

I didn't even pause, "Yes, Zeek, I would."

"In that case it's already too late for you. Shouldn't have waited so long." He started out of the door and got half way down the walk before I called out to him one last time:

"Zeek, what happened to all the other girls? Besides your sister? The other ones that *Scott*," I put emphasis on his name, "got to?" He looked at me strangely, like it should be obvious.

Zeek walked back to me and leaned against the doorframe. He looked down like this was hurting him, and since I believe he think he's right, it may be.

"He killed the annoying ones, and left the others to live their life."

Killed them? I tried to picture Chase hurting so many girls, and I just couldn't.

"So where are they?"

"Doing just that. They're living without him. Blood brides until they die, with no friends, family or love. Some are locked up, went crazy."

"What do you think would have happened to me? If I didn't have Chase and Scott had found me?"

"Doesn't matter Wynter, because Chase isn't Scott, right?" He was taunting me, making me try to believe that he's right. Well it won't work; I know Chase and Scott are two radically different people.

"Right."

16

A Life Altering Decision

It's like trying to win the race,
When you're at start and they're at finish.
Why did you even lace up?
What's the point?
-Nicole Evans

I walked to school Monday morning. The fresh air felt good after being cooped up in the house all day after Zeek left. I stretched, yawned and started walking in the double doors.

"Came to school on time I see Ms. Hayes." The secretary, passing me in the hall, glared over her glasses.

"Just for you." She rolled her eyes but didn't say anything else.

Not my fault school's boring. Anyway if I'm her biggest problem then she has an easy job.

"Knives and Pens," by Black Veil Brides screamed in my ears and I walked down to Zelena's locker. She was standing there getting books out of it and dropping pieces of paper and other random things on top of her locker.

Her normal brown waves were straightened and fell over a white v-neck shirt. I called out to her:

"Lena!" Due to the music I may have been louder than intentioned 'cause a few people besides her turned to look at me; I glared at them.

I looked at Zelena and she looked back, angrily staring at someone behind me. I turned around to see the unlucky recipient of her anger, but no one was there.

I got up to her, "Lena, who you staring at?" But when I looked her directly in the eyes it was made clear.

I'm the unlucky girl.

"What's wrong?" I took a step closer and she held her ground, not backing up but not coming closer to intimidate me, either.

"You." She turned away and continued to pull things out and place them on the locker, mechanically.

I looked; they were *our* things she was taking out of her locker. Drawings that we had made in classes, homework and projects we had ignored together, just a bunch of stuff that meant nothing and everything at the same time.

"What are you doing, Zelena?" She just kept at it, not looking at me.

"Lena." Her being angry with me without telling me why was in turn making me angry too.

"What?"

"What do you mean 'what?' why are you mad at me!?" This wasn't our first fight, but it already seemed like it will turn into our biggest one. Something was different about the way she's going about this.

"Why do you think?" She slammed her locker shut and put all of our things in a brown paper bag.

"I don't know; that's why I'm asking you!" She gave me a disgusted look.

"It's not all about you, Wynter. Don't talk to me until you know." With that she walked away to her first class.

What the hell is that supposed to mean? I walked in the same direction; gym class is going to be awkward as hell. *I don't even know what I did anyway; she could have at least given me a hint. I hate when girls do this, it's their idea of a 'feel bad' punishment or something.*

~ ~ ~ ~ ~

The locker room was packed full of shrieking girls, which didn't help me with trying to think. I saw Zelena laughing with a bunch of them, and it pissed me off. They're as fake as their designer bags and she's acting like they have something really interesting to say. It's pathetic.

I tore off my clothes in a very angry fashion, which ended up being a bad idea. One of my spider bites got caught on my Brokencyde shirt and it hurt a *lot*. Fortunately, nobody saw. I took off my purple zipper skinnies *carefully* and dropped them along with my shirt into the gym baskets we have.

Pulling on my shorts and gym shirt I overheard two of the girls Zelena had been talking to gossiping in low voices:

"Well I heard she has an older boyfriend, he's like *twenty-five* or something!"

"You see the marks on her neck? Most of them time I can't but I have once in a while early in the week and they're really dark!"

"I haven't seen them, what are they?"

"It looked like a hickey at first but I got closer and they're bite marks or something, I mean ew!"

They're talking about me.

Their voices got a little louder, "Ew? I think biting is hot!"

Another, different, girl chipped in, "Not like this, I've seen her neck just once, it looks like an animal bit her, I doubt it's a guy. Let alone a twenty-five year old," *Thank you, mystery girl, you're not a tool like these other chicks,* "I mean why would *any* guy want her? Let alone an older one, puh-lease. She's so . . . weird." *Bitch yes I am.*

"She does wear an awful amount of black, and she skips class like everyday."

"I heard her parents left her and that she, like, lives on her own."

"That would explain why she doesn't get caught with her boyfriend."

"I just told you no guy would want her, why do you keep bringing that up?" *Must be the head bitch.*

"Well if someone did, she's easy."

"I have no doubt about that. And her only friend is Zelena. Poor girl, having to hang out with that freak all day long."

"I just talked to her, they're in a fight."

"Good thing! Maybe now we can get a gang of us to really put her in her place, you know that I heard-"

I stepped around the corner where their previous whispering had pretty much become a normal conversation. Interrupting the Head Bitch mid sentence:

"I heard that she eats fake bitches for breakfast. But that could just be a rumor, like the rest of them are." The girls jumped, having now seen me before I spoke.

"O-Oh, Wynter, we weren't talking about *you*, we were talking about some other g-girl!" A meek freshman hid behind the Head Bitch. In fact, both girls were hiding behind her.

"Really? Who?" She looked down, playing with her fingertips. She was probably only in it for friends. She wasn't real bitch material, a real one wouldn't have backed down so easy.

"*I* was talking about you." HB herself spoke up, throwing a disgusted look at the younger girl behind her.

"Shocker there." I leaned against the lockers, staring them down.

"You think you're *so tough!* Well guess what, you're not!" She gave me a smug look.

"Please, that's how they all start, could you think of something a little more original? Otherwise it's not worth my time."

"You're a slut!" The freshmen tried to redeem herself.

I feigned a hurt look and stepped back, "Easy there, sugar, don't damage my ego too much!" She glared at me but didn't say anything else. *Slut? Such a typical high school insult. Next they'll call me a whore, a hoe, easy, slutty, and not even realize it means the same thing.*

"Don't talk to her that way, whore, you're just jealous of her." The other girl, not HB, spoke up in the freshy's defense.

I so called that one.

"What's there to be jealous of? None of you have got anything I want."

"We're pretty and popular and have, like, a *hundred* times more friends than you do!"

"You can count that high!? Damn, I'm impressed. I thought you could only count up to your IQ, getting past the tens there!" I got flipped off, which wounded me ever so much.

"Prude, jealous, freak." HB threw in.

"Wait, I thought I was a slut? Why do you feel the need to mock me just 'cause I'm not a typical girl like you. You girls are all the same, nothing special here. With your oversized purses, jeans that cost $120, two-for-one insults, and constantly pissy attitudes. What in God's name made you so miserable in life that you get off on making other people feel insignificant?"

"I'll tell you why, because we're better than them, Wynter. We're better than them and we're better than you."

"Oh, you're right. I'm sure you have lots of real friends too, don't you? And nobody's talks behind your back?" The two girls behind HB gave each other guilty glances that she didn't notice.

"Even if they did, which I *know* they don't," more silently exchanged looks, "it's still better than you, who has no friends whatsoever."

"I'd much rather be a loner than look, act, or have anything in common with you. You look just like every other girl in school. Every school has the same girl in it 1000 times over. They dress the same, same style of makeup, same hair color, same attitude, and shop at the same stores. There's no variety in them, which is why there's people like me. I can't even keep track you clones. That's what you are, you know, fake clones."

"You're a bitch."

"Yes, I'm also telling the truth. There's nothing special about you." Freshy looked on the verge of tears; the other girl had nothing to say, mulling it over. HB looked like she got slapped in the face.

"I would consider leaving now, 'cause I *will* kick your ass." Freshy bolted, with the other girl in tow. Only Head Bitch stayed, but once she saw that her minions ditched her, she looked a lot less self-sure.

"Seriously, I'm done, and so are you. Follow your friends." HB complied, because just like every one of the girls like her, she's nothing without her little group backing her up.

Throwing a final insult, "You're alone, you know. If Zelena leaves you, you're gonna be by yourself. Your parents left and she's in the process of leaving. Even if there is a boy, he's just gonna leave too eventually." Then she scampered off. I stamped my feel, making it sound like I was coming after her; she ran away even faster than before.

Ha-ha, I eat bitches.

~ ~ ~ ~ ~

Aside from what little amusement the confrontation brought me, gym was hell. We were playing badminton and I had no partner. Zelena had grabbed a random chick and shot me the evil eye so that option was gone.

"I'll be your partner." Came a voice from behind me. I turned around to find an old acquaintance standing there, awkwardly looking at the birdie.

"Andrew Mota, haven't seen you in forever."

"Yeah, I know, no classes together. I'm just here to make-up one."

"Well thanks, let's get started then, shall we?"

I handed him the racquet and he looked at me like I just gave him a measuring cup and told him to dig a trench.

"How do you play?"

"Just hit it when the other team hits it at us."

"*At* us?" He fingered his gauge nervously; he had about half inch holes in each ear.

"Oh c'mon Andrew, we both know that we're the targets in this school, so yes, at us." He smirked and got into a ready position.

~ ~ ~ ~ ~

We lost. Naturally we weren't trying our best but it didn't help that everyone was aiming for our heads.

It was sort of weird chilling with him again; I haven't really talked to him in like two or three years. We used to be pretty good friends, or at least talked a good deal online about taking over the world. Funny guy, really. But Chase just took over all of my spare time, not that I'm complaining, and we drifted apart. I choose hanging with Chase over hanging with Zelena . . . I mean Andrew.

Oh shit, I just figured out why she's so mad.

I raced to change and run over to her locker before she left for second class.

~ ~ ~ ~ ~

"Zelena!" I cried out her name and raced up to her right before she was going to leave. The brown bag where she had put all of our things earlier this morning was still in her hand.

"You think of anything?"

"Dammit, yeah, I did."

"Well?"

I took a deep breath; running to the lockers wasn't as brisk as I thought it would have been.

"I'm sorry." Her expression didn't change. Normally in one of our fights as soon as the person in the wrong apologized, all was well. But not this time.

"For what Wynter?"

"For putting plans off, for ditching you, for not hanging out, for everything like that." Her expression softened a little, telling me that I was correct in what I was apologizing for.

"Thank you."

"Do you forgive me?" She looked sad.

"There's only one way that I will forgive you. Because this isn't something new, it's been going on ever since you really got involved with him, and it's just getting worse and worse."

"I know, and I'm sorry. I just love him so much, and we're together now!" She didn't look happy for me, "We're together now, so I'll make sure to balance it out between you two."

"Wynter, I'm not looking for balance anymore." Her jaw was set; this was her ultimatum.

"What are you looking for then?"

"A decision. Right here, right now. You get only this time to think."

I froze, *is she thinking what I think she is? No, Zelena would never . . .*

"Choose. Me or him. Right now, you only get one of us. I'm sick and tired of losing you every second to him. Even when you're with me, you're with him. This is your only chance, if you choose him, I'm leaving for good and we're not going to be making up."

I was too shocked to reply for a minute. *What's with her? She does the same thing every single time she has a boyfriend. Every girl does. Why do I have to make a choice, when she's never had to? I can't lose Chase, that's not an option. But Zelena's been my friend for so long . . .*

"You can't do this, Lena. You can't make me choose between my best and only friend and my boyfriend. I love you both."

Her voice shook, "R-right now." The bell above us rang, we were late, not that it mattered right now.

"Zelena you know I can't just choose you over him I can make this work, I-"

She cut me off, "Then you've made your choice. You better hope he's worth it, Wynter, 'cause as of right now, he's all you have."

She was crying and so was I. Zelena started walking away to her class when I tried reaching out to her one last time.

"Wait . . ." she stopped but didn't turn around, "I love you Lena."

Facing away from me, "Not as much as you love him."

Still crying, I watched her go, late, to her second class of the day. As for me, I stood there for five more minutes trying to decide to skip or just sit numbly on a chair for the rest of the day.

I walked to my next class too, I already have summer school for all the days and classes that I've skipped and it's only December, I didn't need anything more on top of that.

17

Numbing Emotion

Tale after tale, of stories and lies,
Told by people so alike and different,
By people so good and so bad,
An avalanche of words and emotions.
-Nicole Evans

We're not friends anymore. This isn't just a high school friendship breakup that'll be back in a few hours. We're really not friends, and we won't be probably ever again.

It's not just losing a friend; it's losing a sister, someone I have confided in over the years, it's like losing a part of me.

When my parent's left, and I was in 7th grade, only thirteen, Zelena was there for me. She slept over for a few weekends with my Aunt Emily and I, and held me when I cried. Nobody but her knew how much it hurt me when I was left like that. She made it better.

I love her with my whole heart, and I can see her being upset, but nothings going to be fixed if she refuses to talk to me. We could have stayed friends, easily. I could have made some room in my schedule, hung with Chase later . . .

But I wouldn't have.

And it's true. I *could* have made time for her, but making time would have meant less time with Chase, so I wouldn't have.

She's right though. No matter how much I love her, and I do a lot, I love him more, I always have. I love them in different ways but I'm in love with him, with Chase. She would have never been able to replace that, and I'm disgusted with her for making me choose. He's a boyfriend and a best friend put together. She is, well was, only a best friend. I just love him more, and I can't help it. It sounds awful, but I couldn't have given him up for her. When she finds someone that just completes her, she'll understand.

~ ~ ~ ~ ~

Monday closed off slow. School dragged on but I didn't really notice it, I was numb. All I did was walk from class to class and sit staring at a different board blankly each hour. Lunch brought me sitting by myself, instead of having her company. I thought about going back to Andrew, but decided not to try and rekindle a friendship that I wouldn't be able to keep up with.

When I got home I took a nap and woke up just in time to make a dinner for myself. Frozen meals, oh boy!

After eating I flopped down on my bed, petting Nightmare.

"Tomorrow will be better Nighty." She purred and hit her head against the palm of my hand, begging for more scratches.

"I love you baby, you'll always be my friend, right? Right, you have no choice!" She walked to the end of my bed, tail in the air, and curled up all ready to sleep.

Tugging my shirt over my head and wiggling out of my pants, I grabbed my PJs. They're my favorite ones, soft dark red with black swirls.

My dad had gotten them for me before he and my mom left. They were a few sizes too big for me so I think he wanted me to keep them and remember him when I was older, or I'm over-thinking and he just didn't estimate my size well.

I got up and turned my light off, racing for my bed so the shadows couldn't get me.

"See you in the morning kitten, Chase is coming home tomorrow!"

~~~~~

Tuesday began as a bright sunny day, so pretty much it was off to an awful start. I had to wear shorts and a tank top as opposed to my normal skinnies and jacket.

Speaking of which, the jacket I normally wore was the best thing I ever bought. I got it at Hot Topic. It's black with a skeleton on it; the skull is on the hood. But that's not even the good part.

There's a wire that plugs into my iPod inside the pocket and headphones run up the inside seem and through the pull strings for the hood. I can listen to music whenever I want and it'll just look like my hoodie strings are messed up. They're machine washable, too.

Back to the point, it's hot out so I had to forsake my wondrous jacket for something more suitable. If I wore my hair down, like I normally do, then nobody would see the bite marks on my neck. They're normally gone, or close to it, by Thursday, they heal fast for some reason, probably has to do with Chase's saliva or something. But the healing doesn't matter much, since he just bites me again on Saturday.

I wonder how those girls in my gym class even saw them anyway. Probably when I put my hair up to change. If I don't then the curls get caught on one of the many necklaces that I normally wear.

I grabbed a pair of black studded shorts and put them on, following that with a loose purple race-back tank top.

"I'll be back later, Nightmare!" I called out, even though she wouldn't be able to answer me.

~ ~ ~ ~ ~

"Welcome home, Wynter." Chase opened his arms and I jumped, so happy to be with him again. He held me close and we kissed, long and hard.

"I missed you!" I laughed into his ear; he chuckled.

"I missed you too, I'm glad to be back." We kissed again and he brought me to the couch, sitting down while I'm still holding onto him.

"Don't leave for such a long time again, okay? Promise! Okay Chase??"

"It was only for a few days!" He caught my eye, "But I promise. Next time I plan on going anywhere, you can come with me."

He kissed my lips again. Then me cheek, then my cheekbone. He trailed kisses down my neck to my collarbone and pressed his teeth against it. I looked past his head right before he was going to bite me and there was Zeek, sitting in a chair facing the back of the couch, watching us.

"Zeek, what are you doing here?" Chase continued to kiss my neck, opting not to bite me. Zeek said nothing.

"Chase, stop . . . Zeek's here." Chase acted like he didn't hear me. Zeek was still silent, just watching us.

"Zeek, you promised you would leave me alone for good last time."

He spoke, "Someone's going to leave you for good, Wynter. Someone besides me, besides your parents, and besides Zelena." I turned to Chase, but found myself alone. I wasn't holding onto him anymore.

"Someone else is going to leave you, and you'll be all alone. Nobody's staying with you Wynter, none of them want you." Zeek's face got bigger until he was the only thing I could see. Swirls of dark colors and Zeek's face, still repeating the same phrase.

"None of them want you Wynter, you'll be all alone. Nobody wants you Wynter, he's going to leave you. He'll leave you forever."

I screamed.

"Zeek get the hell away!!!" I slammed my head on my desk; the teacher and every student in the room looked up at me, startled. Once they saw that I had been sleep talking, they laughed relentlessly.

"Wynter," My teacher chided, "Maybe you should be getting more sleep at home, that way you won't be taking naps in my class."

"Yeah, probably." I yawned, too lazy to say something confrontational. A few students were still giggling so when the teacher turned his back I flipped them off. They grumbled but went back to work.

It's last period, Senior English, I've been getting catnaps in most of the classes I've had today. But I had a nightmare this past one.

What was it about? All I remember is Zeek saying something about me being alone. Chase was in it too I think, not that that's unusual. I never remember my dreams.

I looked at the clock, five more minutes to go, not even. I looked at the quiz in front of me. I wrote next to nothing and doodled a lot. It's on gerunds and participle phrases, which will be useless to me in life as soon as I leave this room.

I handed it in, signing my name with a picture of a cartoon T-Rex. He would know who's it was, I'm the only one who can't get parts of speech and shit like that for her life. I make up for it by working hard on reading assignments. That way I pass the class without having to kill myself studying.

I drew squids battling T-Rex's on some loose paper until the bell rang. The T-Rex's were winning, obviously.

When we heard the end of the day bell everyone walked out, aside from me, 'cause I ran.

Chase is going to be back tonight!

I went smiling to my locker, nearly tripping down the stairs in the process. Switching my iPod to my happy song, "Welcome to the Club," by DJ Manian. I grabbed my homework books, which would lay forsaken on my floor, and slammed the locker shut.

Turning around I saw Zelena walking down the hall. Our eyes met and she turned away, walking angrily in the other direction. I felt my eyes prickle at the sudden, but expected, hostility.

You made the right decision Wynter. You need *Chase in your life. It's painful because you want Zelena in it, but you need him.* I consoled myself because nobody else would. Except when Chase came home, he would talk me through it. I just have to hold out until then. I walked up to the exit, bracing myself for the heat, and headed toward the bus.

～～～～

The monster rolled into my driveway and I raced off, trying to get to my air-conditioned house as fast as possible.

What's this heat!? It's supposed to be cool, cold even, at this time of year. Stupid weather.

Unlocking the front door, I stepped inside to, once again, find broken glass everywhere.

"Damnit, why don't I just get plastic from now on!? That'll sure save a hell of a lot of trouble!"

I saw little toe prints and followed them. Looks like Nightmare cut her paw on some glass when she was making a mess.

It's your fault for leaving the glass on the edge of the counter once you clean them.

"Nightmare, c'mere honey." I did that 'come hither' sound that cats respond to and sure enough she shyly came over. She was favoring her front right paw so I went to where she was and carried her with me to the couch.

"Poor kitten, you step in some glass?" Holding her like a baby I looked at her toe, there was a little piece stuck in it. I touched it, contemplating how to remove it, she twitched uncomfortably.

"Does it hurt? Well you know it's your own fault!" I gave up trying to scold her and cooed to make her feel better.

Grabbing the little piece best I could, I quickly took it out, only to have Nightmare freak and claw my chest.

"Ouch, Night! That hurt, I was just trying to help you!" She scampered around the corner and I heard her flying up the stairs away from me.

"Stupid kitty." I stood up from the couch to clean the rest of the glass when I noticed an oddly placed chair. It was from the dining room, and it was facing towards the back of the couch, like someone had been sitting there, watching it.

I've seen that before . . . but where? Was it in real life? A dream? I never remember dreams so I don't know . . . weird though.

Probably that ghost that *is* in my house. I shrugged and put it back where it was supposed to go.

"Chase will be here later," I said, talking to myself, "Might as well take a nap so I can stay up late talking with him."

I went to nap but kept waking up due to weird dreams. I never remembered any of them, except I knew it was the same one every single time. They were both in it too, Chase and Zeek.

~~~~~

The clock read 8:26pm when I woke up on top of my bed; I had been too tired to even get under the covers. There was a warm body next to mine.

"Chase!" I rolled over and hugged him, opening my eyes.

"You're finally awake! Jeez I thought you had died or something Wynter!" He joked, hugging me back. I poked him, wasn't a dream.

"Nope! I was just waiting for you!"

"Got distracted, didn't you?"

"What do you mean?"

"Broken glass downstairs." Oh shit, I guess I forgot to clean it up before I took my nap.

"Oh, yeah, I was just gonna go get that picked up when I . . ."

"Got distracted." He finished, laughing at me.

"Well we can't all be perfect like you Chase, now can we? Least of all me!"

"Speaking of me being perfect, I cleaned it up and got the glasses away from the edge. What in God's name possessed you to put them there anyway?"

"Not too sure, I can't think of any logical reason why I would in all honesty." I snuggled closer to him, his arm around me. He didn't make fun, rather just held me there.

We lay there a while, not talking. I had turned over at some point and played with his hair. His eyes were closed and he was smiling. I lifted his lip with my finger to see his fangs.

"What *are* you doing?"

"Just 'lookin is all."

"Oh, well that's normal."

"I think it is!" He grabbed my cheeks and pulled them to form a disfigured smile.

"You think this is normal Wynter?" I slapped his hands away.

"That's not what I was doing, stupid head!"

"So you're a senior in high school and calling me a stupid head? Mature, Wynter." I stuck my tongue out at him, to which he rolled his eyes, and cemented the immaturity that I was displaying,

"Speaking of everything," nothing had to relate to this, "How was your visit to your parent's graves?"

He shrugged, "Eh, it was alright. Nothing to report back on, really. Put some flowers down, talked to them awhile, I told them you say hello.

"Thanks." I smiled, knowing that he actually did and wasn't just saying that like most boys would have.

"Mhm. How was your time without me?" I thought back and then Zelena came back to mind. I hadn't thought of her since I left school but thinking about our discontinued friendship brought a fresh wave of emotion. I sniffled.

"That bad?" He frowned, kissing me.

"You can't leave again, okay?" My eyes filled 'cause I was thinking about how much I had given up for him. Not that it's not worth it, but it was still sad.

"Oh Wynter, what happened?" He rolled to his side, hugging me. I cried a little bit, not wanting to be a big baby, which I was becoming a lot of lately.

"Z-Zelena and I ar-ren't friends anymore-e." I could feel myself shaking with new tears having to say that out loud.

"I'm sure it's not that bad, Wynter. It's just a fight is all, you'll make up." He soothed my hair against my head and kissed it.

"N-no. You don't understand. And it's not even just that, Zeek came by." I could feel his muscles stiffen as he heard that.

His voice was hard, clipped, "Did he now? For what reason?"

"I tried to tell him to go away," I shrunk away from him, remembering what happened last time we talked about him. But Chase pulled me close again and kissed my forehead.

"It's okay, you can tell me, I won't be mad."

"He told me he would only leave once he told me his side of the story," Chase once again froze but said nothing, "I listened but it was complete bullshit. The whole thing." *I'll ask him why he lied about Zeek being his half brother later, now's not the time.*

Chase sighed in what seemed to be relief, "So after he told you, he left?" I nodded, "What did he tell you?"

I told him the story that Zeek had told me, except in fewer details and less emotion. Chase just nodded and 'mhm'ed.

"So that's why he's been following me." I shrugged. "I'm sorry I lied to you Wynter, with my story. It's what I've been telling myself for a long time. He's been following me for a while so I think he's gotten me mixed up with someone."

"That's what I told him." Chase smiled like I had done a good job.

"It's a story I came up with a long time ago to make myself feel better and to think of a reason, I don't know why I told you it, I guess I've been thinking it for so long it just seemed real to me."

"So wait . . . are your parents alive then? They killed each other in the story but if Zeek isn't your half brother then how is that possible?" He looked around my room, then at the ceiling.

"It's mostly true. All of that happened but my half-brother died when he was an infant. That's what started the fight that ended up with them killing each other. I just sort of pretended he hadn't to explain why this blood groom was trying to kill me." I digested it.

"That makes sense. So where is your infant half brother in that case?"

"I buried my parents next to where my mother buried him, now I think that may have been inappropriate, but what's done is done I guess."

"What was his name?"

"Sethy. But anyways, how does that relate to Zelena?"

I took a breath, trying to keep myself together, "Well Zeek said that you would leave me, which I know you wouldn't but like a day after he told me that, Zelena did. And I don't know it's just weird and it hurts . . ."

"I understand." And he does, "I love you Wynter."

"I love you too, Chase." We kissed, which as usual turned into a see-how-long-we-can-make-out before-one-of-us-needs-to-breath-again fest.

"I'll love you forever Wynter. All you need is me, 'cause I'll be here no matter what." He whispered into my ear when we stopped kissing and cuddled.

I hugged him closer. There isn't much you can say to that.

"I'm yours Chase, I always will be." I felt his grin against my cheek.

"Speaking of which, how would you feel about . . . actually never mind." He kissed my temple.

"What Chase?"

"Never mind, this probably isn't the right time to talk to you about it anyway . . ." He trailed off again.

"Well you got me interested so now you *have* to tell me!" He 'harrumph'ed but turned on his side, looking me in the eye.

"How would you feel if I asked you . . ." My breath caught, 'cause of what I thought he would say next, "If I asked you if you wanted to become my . . . well, my blood bride?" His eyes were hopeful and my heart beat faster than he had ever made it before.

To be his forever? His sustenance as a blood bride, living with him, loving him, for the rest of an extended life?

I couldn't talk, nothing would come out. I don't think I could say anything to convey my joy to him anyway. I just looked at him; all smiles, and my heart just kept beating faster, praying it wasn't a dream.

He smiled, like he won the lottery, and kissed me.

"Would you do me that favor, Wynter? Would you become my blood bride? Please?" He kissed me again and I nodded, still unable to speak.

"I love you Wynter." I squealed, unable to not say anything but not able to form words.

And I just kept doing it, I squealed more, I hugged him I kissed every inch of his face and I just looked at him.

"Yes," I said when I had finally calmed down enough to speak, "I would."

"We'll have to talk more about the details-" I shut him up with a kiss, details shmetails, I'm going to be with him forever.

I made the right decision.

~ ~ ~ ~ ~

We kissed into the night, spending it together. 'Cause what the hell, we're in love and soon enough I would be his vampire bride. I've lost everything that a girl values to him, and I know it's for the best because he's my everything. He's my forever.

18

New Beginning

I'm not the one you'd want,
I'm not the one you'd save,
But don't ignore me yet,
I'll be the one you crave.
-Nicole Evans

"Would you do me that favor, Wynter? Would you become my blood bride? Please?"

I opened my eyes and shuddered, giggling at the thought that I was going to be with him forever. More thoughts and memories from last night swelled up in my brain and I hid my blush under the covers.

Peaking out I saw Chase sleeping soundly next to me. So I poked him.

"Chase!" Poke, poke, "Psst Psst Psst! Chaaase!" He didn't budge. I wiggled up to his ear, "PPPPPSSSSSSSSSTTTTTTTTTT! Chaaaaaseeeeeee!"

He jumped up like he had been thrown in cold water, "What? What happened, what's going on!?" He looked around, confused.

"Nothing I just wanted to tell you thatttttt, I love you!" He grinned and I saw his fangs.

"You have school today still Wynter, it's," He looked at the clock on my nightstand, "9:32 . . . shit you're really late."

"You're crazy if you think I'm going to school today." I crossed my arms and snuggled closer to his warm side.

"Yeah whatever, it's not like you'll need it in a while anyway." He put his arm around me and it felt safe.

"Will I still go to school?"

"Well I personally don't see the point, we'll be traveling around a lot, unless you want to do the family thing and stay in one place. Do you?" I mulled it over.

We could see the world if we wanted to, but what about my house? Would I just leave it here? And money, what would we do about that?

"Well what would happen to my house? Aunt Emily? Nightmare and Sharkbait? How would we pay for things? How-"

"Should have expected a lot of questions from you Wynter."

"Yes, you should have!" I gave him a peck on the cheek.

"Well your house can stay here, if we turn the heat and everything off then there won't be bills coming so no one will know you're gone."

"Just leave it here? With all my stuff?"

"Think of it as a vacation. We'll go away and come back often enough, that way you can see your Aunt once in a while."

"Nightmare? Sharkbait?" I prodded him; suddenly this was losing some of the high effect on me. There are so many things to worry about.

He looked like he was getting annoyed, "Tell your Aunt that you developed allergies to Nightmare and have her take care of 'em for you or something."

"I can't be allergic to a fish too, and I love them, can't they come with us?"

"Wynter we can't be dragging a cat and a bloody fish everywhere we go!" He yelled, and I got scared, moving a few inches away from him.

His eyes got softer, "I'm sorry, Wyn. I'm tired and hungry," My eyes lit up, "For something a human would eat. Your food gives us enough energy to last until the next blood feeding. Can't have too much blood or it'll pop our veins!" He laughed; it's a warm sound that drew me back to his side.

"Sorry about always asking stuff, I just get worried . . ."

"It's alright, everyone does it. We'll have your aunt take care of Nightmare and Sharkbait and we'll come back often to visit them and her. Sound okay to you?"

I nodded in the affirmative.

"Besides, we don't really have to leave right away."

"Where will we go first? How will we get there? I don't have money."

"Wherever you want. As long as I can feed off of you and there's human food for you to eat, we can go anywhere. Money isn't a problem, either. Vampires can bend people's will slightly, I've told you before. So I can make a person want to give us a free night in their best suite or loan us their car if they're not too strong-willed."

"What if they are? And isn't that stealing?"

"Well if they are then we can't, and will go to the next person. It's not stealing, it's borrowing." He winked and I decided that it really didn't matter much to me anyway.

As long as I'm with Chase, I don't care what we do.

"What happens to me? Like physically? I know vampires don't age past like 20-25, but what about blood brides? Am I going to stay 17 forever?? That'll weird, a 25 year old and 17 year old?"

"That happens more often than you'd think Wynter. But no, you'll probably age a little more but not much. When you're changed, venom is pushed into your veins, stopping the developing process slowly. You might make it to eighteen or nineteen."

"That's not so bad I guess." He kissed my ear, it was loud.

"I think you'll be perfect." I hugged him, smiling as much as I could hold.

"Lets go eat, I'll see if I can make something without burning down my kitchen!" His face lost some color,

"How about I make something, okay? Frozen dinners are your specialty, I'll make the real food." I grumbled, but he was right, I'm a cooking disaster. He got up out of bed and I blushed, waiting for him to change.

~ ~ ~ ~ ~

A few hours later we had eaten and gotten ready for the day. It was cold and sunny. Winter was upon us. I've never celebrated Thanksgiving. Aunt Emily always goes away with her boyfriend of the year, Zelena and her family visit relatives, and I can't cook so I don't wanna be embarrassed trying in front of Chase. So fall fades into winter rapidly, with no holiday in between.

"It's cold as a bucket of ice!" Chase laughed, watching me looking at my breath.

"Ice tends to be cold. It was really hot yesterday, I don't know how it got to be so cold so fast."

"That's what I'm saying! Jeez it's freezing out now but yesterday I thought I would die."

"Maybe it was a last ditch attempt before winter comes in. The last hoorah."

"I guess . . . when will it snow Chase?"

"I'm not the weather man, I don't know. We can check when we get back to your house if you want, alright?"

"Mhm! I hope soon, I want this place to be coooovered in snow! It's pretty."

We're walking into the woods, to our secret hideout. When the snow falls we'll have to go in from a different way, so nobody can follow our footprints and find it.

"You've always looked beautiful in the winter."

"Don't make fun of my name, loser!" I stuck out my tongue and he pretended to grab for it.

"I'm serious! You do. Plus your hair shows up well against the white. It's like looking at a black and white picture. Your hair is black, the snow is white, your skin is whiter than the snow," I hit him; he always makes fun of my albino like skin.

"Well it is, you wear SPF 85 or something like that."

"I don't want skin cancer!" I stuck out my tongue again but skipped away before he could try to grab it.

"I'm surprised it even exists Wynter."

"It's special, like me!" He laughed. I'm not really an albino, just especially pale.

"Would you rather I have pale skin or get a fake tan and be orange?"

"Fake tans are disgusting, not to mention you *will* get cancer if you try it."

"I know, which is why I don't fake tan, hell I don't even real tan for that matter."

"Oh I'm aware."

We walked in silence, holding hands the whole way. Even just a little touch like that was special, and my hand burned. Every sense was ablaze when I was with Chase. It never diminished and I never got used to it, which made it better. My love won't fade, I feel too much when I just think about him.

"Chase," we're sitting under our climbing tree now, the one that sticks out like a sore thumb among the rest, "When will you turn me?"

He soothed my hair, "When do you want to be?"

I blushed, "In all honesty, right now. Will you? Will you please? I want to be yours forever!" He smirked.

"Oh trust me, you'll be mine forever." He had a semi-evil look on his face; I think he was teasing me.

"Good, 'cause I could never love anyone like I do you." He kissed my hand.

"I know, Wynter, I know." We sat in silence for a little while before I ruined it again.

"So when will you change me, if not right now?"

"Tonight. If that's all right? I know you can't wait and I see no reason to." I could feel my heart beating super fast and I just *know* I'm blushing.

"The sooner the better Chase!" We kissed. It was a sweet kiss, the first of many more to come.

How did it come to this so fast? Just yesterday I could only dream of being with him forever. Today I can say that I will be. And tomorrow will seal the deal. It's a dream, his love is a dream. I'll treasure every second I have with him.

"Will it hurt?" I asked but I didn't really care. I would take years of torture and it would be worth it in the end if I got him.

"Only if you think me biting you hurts, and I know for a fact that you don't." We blushed and I touched my neck unconsciously.

"Will the venom? Just curious."

"Well it's never hurt anyone before." As soon as the words left his lips he went ridged and gave me a sideways glance.

"What do you mean? You've changed someone before?" He looked lost, grabbing at words in his head.

"No." More thinking, but to me, he looks awfully guilty of something.

"Chase, have you?"

"No, no, I just misspoke. Or wasn't clear." His eyes were calming down, a story behind them.

"I know people who have been changed and vampires who have changed them, and they all said that it didn't hurt in the least."

I calmed as well, relieved that I was still the only one, "Oh, okay that's good."

"Are you scared?"

"No, I would have taken pain but it's a bonus that there won't be any."

"Mmm. That's true."

We sat under the tree talking about everything and nothing at all. Kissing, hugging and just chilling. It got to be late afternoon somehow and we ended up going back to my house.

I need to call Zelena and get her to talk to me . . .

~~~~~

"I'll meet you at Nightingale Park, 9 o'clock." He looked at me with love in his eyes. Love and a glimmer of other emotions, but I didn't care about them.

"Why in the park? Why not here?" He looked lost for a reason as to why.

"I just like that place, so why not?"

It is a nice park. Especially at night, beautiful.

"Alright. Where in there? It's pretty big, plus I don't wanna go in alone, there are a lot of homeless people sitting around, could get sketchy at night."

"I would never have you go in alone, I'll meet you at the front entrance and we can take a walk together. No way am I just having you go in, that's not safe. I love you too much to have you in danger."

"I love you too, I know you'll make me safe!" I jumped up into his arms, savoring his scent, his touch, how he held me.

"I get you forever, right Chase?"

"I get *you* forever Wynter." He answered my question with a statement of his own.

"I'm going to go now, get my stuff packed together, I'm going to move it in here while we're gone, that okay?"

"Yes, but are we leaving right away?"

"No, probably stay here for a few weeks, but there's no reason for me to keep my things outside when I can just keep them in here with you." He smiled warm and suggestively, I giggled nervously.

"Okay. I'm going to call Aunt Emily over to take Nightmare and Sharkbait and their things, just to get that out of the way."

"Sounds good, I love you Wynter."

"I love you too, Chase." He walked out the front door.

Next time I see him he'll be ready to make me his forever, I thought.

Time to call Aunt Emily to pick up my little kitten and the fish. Then I have to try to get through to Zelena. I have to at least talk to her before I get changed . . .

~ ~ ~ ~ ~

It took some time explaining to Aunt Emily as to why she needed to take the cat. I told her I thought I was coming down with allergies to her and didn't want to take the chance. She had asked:

"What about the fish? Why do you want to give me that too?"

"His name is Sharkbait, and Nightmare needs company, she'll be lonely without me. So Sharky will remind her that I love her!"

My aunt sighed, "You have a weird way of looking at things, don't you Wynter?" I grinned.

"I always have!"

"Alright well you've given me the food, litter box, toys and all the fish stuff so I think I'll get going. Anything else you need?"

"I'll get Nightmare, she's in my room."

"Okay."

"Thank you very much for all this and everything else you've done over the years." She smiled at me.

"Not a problem honey, not a problem at all."

I waved to her as she got into the car, I would be seeing her again soon. I waved bye to Sharkbait and went upstairs to get Nightmare.

Finding her asleep on my bed, "Oh baby, I'm going to miss you so much." She meowed, stretched, and walked over to me lazily.

I scratched her head; "I wanna take you with me!" I cried, it was hard to say goodbye to her, my little kitten, even knowing that I would see her soon enough.

"I'm going to miss you," I repeated, "I love you Nightmare."

I walked downstairs with her in my arms and placed her in a cage. Her gray blue fur stood on end at being put in such a confined place. I stroked her soft paw through the bars.

Still crying, "I love you Nighty. So much. And I'll come visit you when I can, promise. She seemed to know what was going on and let out a small, sad meow.

"Goodbye Sharkbait, Nightmare." I told Aunt Emily goodbye again and she drove off.

Done recalling the memory, I felt my eyes prickle. I grow very attached to my animals, which makes it hard to see them go with her.

"She'll take care of them." I spoke to an empty house.

I've given up so much for him. Not just my heart, mind and body. But my pets, possible friendship with Zeek, and Zelena too . . . It's all going to be worth it though.

Then, after mustering up some courage, I got to the phone to dial a number I knew by heart.

"What?" came the voice on the other end.

"Zelena, can we talk?"

"No, I told you that we're done. I'm not looking for an enemy but I'm not looking to rekindle a torn up friendship either."

"Please, just for a little, maybe you can understand-"

"I can't and won't Wynter. You choose him, you made your choice. You may as well be dead 'cause that's what you are to me." She hung up.

I cried, it was coming to me easier these past few months.

"Well then," I said, wiping my tears, "It's just me and him versus the world."

~ ~ ~ ~ ~

8:30 came around and I figured a twenty minute walk would put me at the park. I went out the front door and looked at my house, the place I grew up. Where my parents raised me, and then left me. Where Zelena and I had hung out until she choose a future without me. Where Zeek had almost become a friend before I made him leave. Where Chase asked me to stay with him forever.

Next time I'm here, I'll be Chase's blood bride.

I took a final look, shut the door and started walking. Not looking back once.

"Too bad I will never love you back."

19

This is the End

It started with the screaming,
But no one could hear it,
It ended with the gunshot,
But no one's left to fear it.
-Nicole Evans

I dressed myself in my mourning finest; a black gothic Victorian style dress. I did my eye make-up the usual black and purple, put on heavy as ever. My black curls spiraled down my back. The self-induced scratches and cuts on my arms and face from that morning at the park were left uncovered for the world to see.

Walking through the snow in black lace flats, I made my way to our pond. Memories pushed me forward and I got lost in them.

~~~~~

I woke up in a white room, dressed in a checkered hospital gown. I saw my left hand cuffed to the bed, an IV in it. Scratches were all over my arms and I could feel them on my face as well.

A doctor came in the room.

"Ah, so I see you're up. Are you calm enough for me to order this removed?" He came over and nudged the handcuff with his clipboard.

I looked at him dumbly, still unable to think of anything but him.

"Looks like it, I'll go get the officer." He left for a moment and came back with a man in blue. He gave me the weary eye and un-cuffed me. Then turning away from me, he looked at the doctor.

"You can go back to the station now, we can handle it from here." I saw the belt in front of me and knew what I had to do.

"With all due respect Doctor, I should take her back with me." I bumped his hip and he jumped, afraid I had gone after him.

"Watch it little lady, don't bump an armed officer."

Armed my ass. I moved my un-cuffed hand under the hospital beds sheets.

"No, the tox screen was negative and my employees have not filed a law suit against her. There is no reason for you to."

The officer grumbled off, leaving me looking at the doctor, who was looking right back.

"So, do you know why you're here?" I did. Tears leaked out from the corners of my eyes.

"I can see you're scared," He misread my emotions, "Well you're alright now, safe from everyone and everything . . . except yourself that is."

I looked at him, saying nothing. What could I say?

Chase, Chase, Chase.

He's gone.

I'm nothing without him and he's gone.

"I want to refer you to a physiatrist," that got my attention and I looked at him more intensely.

He sighed, "Boyfriend?" I nodded. But oh, was it so much more than that.

"Thought so, look I know it seems like the worst thing to happen to you in your life, but it's not. I have a twenty-five year old who went through all of that. But she's happily married now, and in the future, you will be too."

No I won't.

Chase is the only one for me, without him I'm nothing. Useless. Trash. I was never fit to love him.

"If I get your name and address and you promise to call this number, I can discharge you right now."

I gave him a fake name and number, knowing that there was no way I would be in touch with him, a physiatrist, or anyone else for that matter, ever again.

He dropped a brown bag at the foot of the bed and took the IV out, bandaging it.

"These are your clothes, you may leave as soon as you want, Summer."

Summer; the first name that came to mind. How ironic, the first thing that comes to mind is the opposite of what I am . . .

"Remember that number!" He called over his shoulder and then he was gone. Small town police officer, small town hospital. I was sure they were breaking hundreds of laws by letting me go as soon as I woke up, but it just worked out better for me.

I changed as quickly as I could and soon I was gone as well.

The hospital was right near the park, the damn park, the place where everything ended. I knew my way home so I started out.

~ ~ ~ ~

The trees loomed in front of me. All of them were as bare as death. It was snowing and though I had no jacket I didn't feel the cold, not really.

~ ~ ~ ~

I got home and planned. I need a shower first, if I'm going to do this, I'll do it right.

I took one and started getting ready. I had a dress that I bought for no reason a while ago. Took months of saving but I knew in the back of my mind that I would need it. Now's the time.

~ ~ ~ ~

The officer was incredibly stupid. When he was talking to the doctor all I had to do was hit him a little bit. Just a tap really and he didn't notice me take this out.

I held up the shiny object to the winter sun.

"It's beautiful." I kissed the side.

The holster had been worn and wouldn't have been in very good shape to begin with. I live in a small town, he works in a small town, there's no reason to waste money to have incredibly safe holsters on the officers that see no action.

I arrived at the pond. I looked at my footprints from where I had come. I walked up to the edge and looked down.

A thin layer of ice covered the water. So thin that if I touched it, it probably would have broken.

Perfect.

I smiled and turned away from the water, standing on the edge.

"You're beautiful." I said to the shiny object again. "So beautiful . . . you know I'm beautiful too. Chase thinks I am. He didn't leave me, 'cause he thinks that I'm beautiful. I'm his blood bride, he didn't leave me. I just have to go to another place to find him is all." I smiled, 'cause I know it's true.

I held up the officers missing gun and saw how it looked against the snowing sky. The sun peeked through some clouds, glinting off the barrel.

I held it up to the side of my head, poised to go to the other place and find Chase.

"This is a punishment," I spoke to myself, "I have to give something up for him, for Chase. So we can be together forever! I shouldn't punish my head, my brain; I'll punish my heart. I'll sacrifice my heart so I can go on and find him." I lowered the gun from my temple to my left breast.

"I can give this up to be with him. I really can!" I kissed the barrel of the gun once more and started crying.

Because I know no matter how crazy I may have become, I can't fool myself. I know Chase isn't waiting for me on the other side. He didn't die. But I'm about to.

"He isn't waiting for me, he doesn't love me, but I can pretend that he's there, in love with me, for just a little longer."

With a sudden stroke of passion, bravery, and depression, I whipped the gun to my heart and pulled the trigger.

~~~~~

I'm falling backwards into the water. I can feel my body breaking through the thin layer of ice, like I knew it would.

An icy shock blasted through my clothes and joined the pain that was in my heart. I would not die instantly; I don't deserve to die instantly. I deserve to suffer for my stupidity. To bleed out in this water. The cold would only prolong my suffering. Good.

Why, oh why didn't I listen to Zeek? No . . . why didn't he come sooner? I was already in too deep by the time he arrived. There was nothing to save me, no one to save me. Nobody that cared enough to.

The pain in my heart, both emotional and physical was near unbearable.

But I deserved every second of it.

Would I have fallen for him anyway, had Zeek come right after I met him?

Probably.

There's no helping it, Chase is an unstoppable force of nature. And I'm just one of the girls. Just one of many that played his game.

I'm crying under water, each tear is a bullet from my eyes.

I can see my blood escaping and mixing in front of me.

My dress, so heavy, pulls me to the bottom.

"Wynter, you made your choice. You may as well be dead 'cause that's what you are to me."

"Would you become his blood bride if he asked you to be? In that case it's already too late for you."

"You will always belong to me, but I will never be yours. Did you really think that you were good enough to deserve the love of a vampire?"

Why? Why do all the closest, the ones that matter, leave me? My parents left me, Zeek left me, Zelena left me, and Chase . . . he left me too. I gave him everything and he took it, took all of it until I had nothing left to give him but my heart, my soul. Then he took those too and ran away laughing.

My eyes are getting heavy and all I can feel is the sharp needles of cold pain along with the explosion in my heart. Where my heart used to be.

My last thought was this,

I'm yours forever, Chase.

. . .

And then I died.

Epilogue

Part One

Would it have made a difference? If I had come to save her earlier on? Would she have lived and thrived in due time? Grown up and gotten married? Raised a family?

"Most likely not." I answered my own question out loud. It's hard, seeing them go through the pain. Wynter has been the worst to see so far, aside from my sister, Kaylee. She gave up everything, and I could see that. Lucius worked longer and harder on this one, and it sure as hell paid off.

None of the other girls killed themselves before. Wynter was the first. I was too late to stop her, but even if I had she would have found another way. I couldn't baby-sit her forever. There will be other girls.

Lucius will never stop. He's been at it for so long; I've seen him take another every few years. It keeps him alive, the first blood of a blood bride. The first blood is supposed to sustain a vampire for even longer than normal blood would. He's just taking that and making a game out of it.

I dropped my finished cigarette into the snow. Looking down over the edge of the pond I saw blood in the water and a dark mass at the bottom.

"Shit. I have to do better." I was getting better by striking fear into Lucius' heart, but clearly I wasn't good enough. Not yet. Lucius, his real name. He told me right before he thought he would kill me once. He's old, so very old, and that's his birth name. The bullshit story he tells every girl about his parents killing each other? *He* killed them. Don't know why . . . yet.

I learn a little more about him every time we meet, every time I get closer to getting him for good.

He refuses to meet friends of his present victim because he's worried that they'll end up hunting him like I do. Like I always will until he's as dead as my sister is, as Wynter is.

I'll continue to hunt him; I'll avenge them all.

Epilogue

Part Two

It's a beautiful day. Sunny and hot but patches of shade so it doesn't irritate my eyes. I felt her blood coursing through my veins. I feel young again, and I'll stay fit for a long time with this blood. Her love was so strong, so pure. It was the best job I've ever done.

And that brat Zeek couldn't do shit to stop me. Oh he tried, but he's still nothing against me. The only reason I didn't kill him is because I hadn't fed in a while when I saw him, and I was weaker than I normally would be.

I laughed out loud to myself.

"Humans are so foolish."

I kept walking along the street, far away from the state where I left Wynter, so I need not worry about Zeek being around the bend. It'll be a good few months before he gets an inkling as to where I am, and by then I'll already have another girl wrapped around my pinky finger.

And there she was. My next victim. Walking towards me. They all start off the same, tired and unsure of themselves. I meet them, befriend them and help them. Soon enough, they're madly in love with me. I'm that good.

The girl had long sleeves, and in this heat it was probably to hide either self-injuries or marks of the abused. Her brown hair was straight and covered her eyes, which were glued to the ground.

So broken, I thought to myself, *Does Daddy hit you? Does Mommy drink? Good. All the better for me, she needs my support, and I'll give it to her.* I laughed again.

I walked faster and moved in closer, giving her less room to get by me.

We collided, like I planned.

"Oh!" She cried out, losing her balance, but I caught her. She looked up into my eyes and swooned. Perfect.

"Oh, I'm so sorry miss . . ."

"M-my name's Kathryn. I'm sorry, I wasn't looking where I was going . . ."

"Not at all, I was the one moving too fast. Kathryn . . . what a gorgeous name, for a gorgeous girl." She blushed, "Here, are you hurt?" She shook her head.

"Well if you would allow me, please let me walk you home, so no more misfortune falls on you." She looked about how old Wynter had been. Maybe older, but much more insecure.

"S-sure. U-um I'm sorry, what's your name-e?" She stuttered.

I decided in a nanosecond and told her, "I'm dreadfully sorry, allow me to introduce myself. My name's Zach."

And here we go again.

The End

LaVergne, TN USA
06 December 2010
207684LV00002B/2/P